KEEPERS OF THE KINGDOM

Maile Spencer Honolulu Tour Guide Mysteries

Kay Hadashi

Keepers of the Kingdom
Maile Spencer Honolulu Tour Guide Mysteries
Kay Hadashi. Copyright 2020. © All Rights Reserved.
Revised contents, July 2021.
Cover art by author adapted from Kingwood Creations.

ISBN: 9798696128313

This is a work of fiction. Characters, names, places, dialogues, and incidences are used factiously or products of imagination. Any resemblance to actual persons, businesses, events, or locales, unless otherwise denoted as real, is purely incidental. No part of any character should be considered real or reflective of any real person, living or dead. Information related to current events should be considered common knowledge and can easily be found in real life.

www.kayhadashi.com

Chapter One

On that Friday morning, sunrise felt more like midnight. When Maile Spencer's alarm clock rang at 'way-too-early' o'clock, she gave it a slap, sending it to the floor. The extra money she was spending lately on new alarm clocks was paying off, because this one didn't break. But in spite of the alarm, she didn't get up for the long run she had planned. Instead, she turned over and let the wonder of sleep drift through her mind again.

When Maile finally did wake up, it wasn't to the racket of the Mendozas treating the building to their usual eight AM argument. It was, in fact, quiet. Getting her clock from the floor, she discovered it was long after the time Rosamie would slam a door or break a dish. Putting the clock back on the end table where it belonged and sweeping hair from her face, Maile sat on the side of the bed. Right then, she wanted the scent of fresh-brewed coffee in her nose, followed by the first few luxurious sips of dark brown wonderfulness.

"I have to get one of those coffeemakers that automatically turns itself on."

Already running late for the day, she needed to hurry through a shower and dressing, followed by rushing through a single mug of tea. She had plans to grab a quick meal at a local diner, a splurge but necessary since her cupboards were bare. Throwing what she needed for that day's tour into her bag, she made a fast break for the door, leaving her room in a mess when she left.

Being a tour guide dropped many surprises into her life, but the predictable unreliability of her car was not one of them. Needing to rely on her car that day, she'd fired up the engine the night before, and celebrated when it continued to run with very few threats from her. She'd even taken it to the carwash and vacuumed the interior. When she got to the sidewalk and turned the corner to where she left her car parked the evening before, she got her first surprise of the day. The hood was up, and she saw the legs of a man who was bent over the engine compartment.

"Hey! Get away from my car!" Maile shouted as she hurried down the sidewalk. It wasn't much of a car, and often hoped it would get stolen, but not on a day when she needed it. The man stood up straight and looked at her. When she saw who he was, she stopped running. It didn't mean she wasn't worried. He was a lawyer she had come to know in the last few months, also a friend, someone that spent time intruding upon her daydreams. "Oh, it's you. What're you doing to my car?"

"Maile, how are you?" David Melendez, Honolulu's priciest lawyer asked. He was tall, dark, and handsome, with wavy black hair and an easy smile. She'd never seen him in anything other than an expensive suit. Today, dressed in a grubby T-shirt with the name of his alma mater on the front and a pair of running shorts, he was attractive in a whole new way.

"I'm fine." She looked into the engine compartment. A couple of parts had been removed and were on the sidewalk getting suntans. "What're you doing to my car?"

"You've been complaining it hasn't been running right, so I came by to take a look," David said. "From the way you described the ignition problems, you need new spark plugs. I haven't seen a car with old-fashioned ignition like this in years."

Maile picked up a grubby spark plug with fingertips. "Yeah, great, but who asked you to do all this?"

He seemed taken aback by the question. "Well, no one. Just trying to keep you mobile."

"How long will it take to put it back together again? Because I have to pick up someone at the airport, and I have an errand to run first."

"Can it wait?" David asked, as he went back to work on the car.

"Not really. In fact, it's your niece Thérèse that I'm picking up at the airport. She's coming in a few hours before her mother gets here from Maui," Maile said. The tradewinds were steady and strong that morning, tossing her hair across her face and fluttering her sheer silk scarf. Otherwise, she was dressed in a blouse and loose shorts for what she suspected would be an active day. "My job today is to hang out with an energetic ten-year-old. And just as a reminder, I need my car to drive her around town. How much longer will it be?"

"Two minutes." David set down his tool and climbed in the driver's seat. When he stuck a key into the ignition, Maile checked her key ring.

"Where'd you get a key for my car?"

"You had a key in one of those little magnetic boxes stuck under the bumper," he said. "Same place everybody puts one of those, and the first place a car thief will look."

"Who'd want to steal this old piece of junk?"

David quit turning the key in the ignition when the engine didn't respond. "I don't understand. Everything is adjusted and set properly," he said, now looking at the engine again.

"See that round black thing? Give that a slap," Maile said. "Sometimes that makes it go."

"I'm trying to fix it so you don't have to hit it into submission," David said. He began taking things apart again. "This might take a while. Want to borrow my car to go to the airport? By the time you get back, I should be done with this."

"You've never seen me drive."

"What's that mean?" he asked, still working on engine parts.

"See all the dents and scratches on it? I put all those there. If you look in the glove compartment, you'll find a stack of traffic tickets. Very few of which are my fault, by the way. Is there anything you can do about those?"

"Yes, tell you to pay them before a judge signs a warrant for your arrest."

"They can do that? Arrest someone for unpaid tickets?"

"If it's elapsed the time and remains unpaid, they can do it with only one ticket. Or a bounty hunter can pick you up and take you in. That only adds to the fine, instead of reducing it."

"That actually happens? That's not just reality TV stuff?"

"Yes, it's done all the time," David said, as he tried the ignition again. This time, the engine turned over and the car started with a backfire.

"Hey, it runs good!" she said. "You fixed it."

"That sounds better?" he asked.

Maile got in the car and snapped her seatbelt. "Hasn't run this good in years."

After David collected tools and slammed the hood down, he went to the window. He seemed nervous. "Are you busy tomorrow?"

"So, that's what this is all about? You fix my car and then ask me out on a date?"

"No, it's not like that." David laughed. "Okay, maybe it is. Are you interested?"

"Tomorrow, I have a wedding at noon, and then the reception for the rest of the afternoon. After that, I'll be exhausted."

"How about breakfast?"

She looked at him suspiciously. "Breakfast?"

"As in drop by and pick you up for breakfast in a restaurant?"

"Having breakfast with the bridal party. Sorry. All about us girls tomorrow."

"Another time?" he asked.

"Let me ask you this. Do you believe in your mechanical skills?"

David looked uneasy. "I'm a lawyer, not a mechanic."

"Tell you what. If my car holds up all day, you have yourself a date for next weekend."

"You're on." He gave her arm a squeeze. "Drive carefully."

***

Running late because of the car repairs, and whatever it was that happened at the end, Maile needed to hurry to her appointment. She found a parking place in front of the Chinatown salon and hurried in, dodging a few autumn raindrops. The tropics were never cold at sea level, but seasonal changes could be seen in the dark clouds that came over the Ko'olau Range that split Oahu in half. Daily temperatures that would be in the high eighties in the summer relaxed ten degrees in the so-called winter months.

She hadn't expected to see her there, but a new acquaintance was in the salon, mostly hanging around and chatting. Her smile came easier than she thought it would.

"Binh, how are you?"

One of the stylists rushed over before Binh could answer. "Little Binh getting stronger every day!"

The young Vietnamese girl shrugged off the woman she called Auntie. Barely smiling, she said, "I'm fine. Nice to see you again, Maile. I saw your name on the schedule. What are we doing today?"

"I'm in a wedding tomorrow, and I'm supposed to get nails like these. I also need a facial and my brows shaped." Maile got out a sheet of paper of what needed to be done, complete with intricate diagrams. "Exactly like these pictures or I'm in trouble."

"Facial and brows are easy. We can do everything at the same time," Binh said.

Without work to do, the hairstylist wandered off. Binh and another young woman named Lin discussed the instructions for a moment.

"You'll need artificial nails for that," Lin said.

"Oh. You can't do that to my real nails?"

Binh took Maile's hand and examined her fingers. "No way. You shouldn't chew."

"I don't. Not very often, anyway."

Lin led Maile to a nail station and started prepping her nails for acrylics. While that went on, Binh barked orders at another young woman who came over and eased Maile back in the chair. Five minutes later, Maile was being double-teamed, brows being stringed and cuticles being excised, with a conversation taking place over her in Vietnamese.

"I need to go open the restaurant," Binh said, of the family's other business right next door. "Come over for a bite when they're done."

Maile agreed, but she knew she would be in too much of a hurry if she wanted to meet Thérèse's flight on time. She was the daughter of a Maui VIP, a well-known surgeon and popular mayor. She was also paying Maile a lot for a few hours of what was basic babysitting duty framed as a tour.

After an hour of tedious work and very little conversation, one last layer of solution was spread on her face and her fingers were put in a brightly lit dryer. Looking in a mirror aimed at her face, Maile's complexion was paler and her brows were half the size they'd been when she walked in.

"Okay?" the brow artist asked.

Maile checked the diagrams. Her brows matched perfectly. "Looks good, thanks. Anything you can do about the size of my nose?"

The brow artist took something from a drawer. It was a business card for a Chinatown plastic surgeon. "Good doctor. Fix up everybody around here."

Not wanting to be rude by refusing it, Maile tucked the card in a pocket. "I'll keep it in mind."

While Lin and the brow artist put away their tools, one of the hairstylists strolled over.

"Big date?" the stylist asked.

"Wedding."

The stylist beamed. "Yours?"

"No, thank goodness. My friend. I'm a bridesmaid."

The stylist pretended to understand but Maile could tell she didn't. Lin did a quick translation. The stylist quickly smiled again. "Want new haircut?"

As always, on the rare occasion when she got her nails done professionally, Maile had to fend off a scissors-happy stylist. She'd worn her hair long all of her life and wasn't about to change it on a whim. As it was, she had another diagram of how it was supposed to go into a French twist for the ceremony. "Not this time. I need to stick to the plan and look the way I'm supposed to look for Lani's wedding tomorrow."

When Lin didn't bother translating for her, there was confusion on the stylist's face. While Maile continued to hold her nails in the dryer, the stylist went to a poster on the wall. "This one good for you. Try it today?"

Keepers of the Kingdom

Maile gasped internally when she saw it. "I wonder what Lani would do if I showed up with that on my head tomorrow?"

Looking heartbroken that she didn't have a customer, the stylist wandered off to find a perch in front of a whirling fan. Lin turned off the nail dryer and led Maile back to the front. When Maile tried to pay, Lin waved her off. "No need."

"Why not?"

The stylist answered. "My niece...little Binh..." She put her arms up and made muscles in her biceps. "Because you. If no you, she would be..." She made a fake dead face that looked a little too realistic. "No more ever pay for you here. Or at restaurant. Always free for you."

Putting that to memory, she thought of other services she could have done when it came time to remove the fake nails. "Have to leave giant tips instead, though."

Skipping out on going to the restaurant next door, Maile raced to the airport. Just as she was parking, she got a call from the bride in the next day's wedding.

"Lani, I just came from the nail salon." She admired her new set of nails and wondered if she could afford them more often. "They look great. I've never had nails this long before. Not that they're real."

"Maile! It's terrible!"

"What's wrong?"

"I've never been so...it's terrible!"

"Wait. Slow down and tell me what's wrong. Is there something going on with Ronald?"

"No, he's fine. Where are you? Will you be here soon?"

"I just have an errand to run. I'll be there as soon as I can."

Maile couldn't imagine what was so wrong that her friend was nearly hysterical. Maybe a bridesmaid had been in the suntan booth too long, or one of them had gained a few pounds and no longer fit into her gown. She remembered her own wedding from four years before, and how she had freaked out when she woke up the morning of her wedding with a bad case of acne on one cheek. No longer wearing her wedding ring and months since the last time since she'd even seen her ex-husband, it all seemed rather silly.

"Yes, it's the duty of the bride to decompensate if everything isn't perfect."

The airport terminal was a busy place, with arrivals coming from neighboring islands and from the mainland. The passengers from Thérèse's flight from Maui were just coming into the terminal. The girl was carrying a brown paper bag when she came through.

"Hey! You made it! How was the flight? Are your arms tired?" Maile asked.

"Old joke, Maile."

"Yeah, I guess so. I've always thought it was funny." Maile led the girl toward the exit. "What's in the bag?"

"I dunno. Sack lunch, I guess."

"Your mom didn't have to send a lunch. Oh, yeah. You guys are vegetarians. What'd she make for you?"

"Peanut butter sandwich, carrot sticks, fruit cup, juice box. Same thing as always."

"Sounds like what I always got," Maile said. "What's on your itinerary?"

"I dunno. Hang out at your house?"

"Maybe for a while. I have something kinda fun to do first, though. Is that okay?"

"As long as it's not looking for dead guys at Diamond Head, okay with me. What is it?"

"Well, I'm in a wedding tomorrow, and this morning we have the practice for it. Want to watch?"

Thérèse stopped walking and beamed at Maile. "Your wedding?"

"Um, no, thank goodness. My friend. It'll only take about an hour or so. Kawaiaha'o Church is really pretty and historic. If you get bored, there's a graveyard to inspect, and some old mission houses next door we can visit. Then the rest of the day is ours."

"Until my mom gets here for her meetings."

"Oh, yes. Big state government meetings this weekend. Not much fun for you."

"Maile?" someone said from nearby.

Maile looked for who it was but didn't recognize anyone.

"Maile!" a girl shouted. "There you are!"

Maile scanned the crowd again, only to find a girl wearing a knapsack. It took a moment for her memory to put a name to the face, a guest on one of her tours a few months before. "Samantha? It's nice to see you. Are you on vacation here again?"

"I guess so."

"Where're the others? Your parents?"

The girl looked worried, her expression darkening. "At home, I guess."

Maile looked around the busy terminal, still trying to figure out what was going on. "Oh. Are you here on a group tour with other kids?"

Samantha's lip started to quiver. "Um, no, just me."

Maile crouched down to eye level with the girl. "How can you be here by yourself? Where's your mother?"

That's when the dam of tears burst on Samantha's face. "She's at home."

"At home? How did you..." Maile took the girl in her arms for a hug. "Does she know you're here?"

Samantha shook her head. "I came by myself."

Maile got tissues from her bag to wipe tears. "How did you do that?"

"The internet. I was able to buy a ticket and put a message with it that a kid would be flying alone."

"But your parents would've needed to check you in at the airport in...where do you live again?"

"Ohio."

"How were you able to find the right terminal and check in?" Maile asked.

"The taxi driver helped me. I gave him a big tip. Is a dollar a big tip?"

"For a kid. You would've needed to disembark from one flight to get on another. How did you know how to do that?"

"The airplane stewardess lady got a ticketing lady to take me to the right terminal for the next flight."

"Does your mother know you're here? Or anyone at home?" Maile asked.

The girl shook her head. Maile could see the strain in her eyes, maybe not getting much sleep during the long flights, worried and homesick.

"Who were you waiting for? Do you have family here? Who's coming to pick you up?"

"Just you."

"What? How long have you been sitting here waiting for me?"

"I guess an hour. I tried calling your tour company, but the office isn't open yet."

Maile stood. "Okay, seriously, you can't just hop onto an airplane and fly somewhere, and then expect someone to come pick you up."

"I did," Thérèse said. She'd been standing there listening to Samantha's tale. "You picked me up."

"Yes, but you were sent by your mother from the next island over, took a short flight, and your mother arranged with me for your pickup. She even called and verified with me that I was still available before she let you get on the plane. That's a lot different from Samantha taking two long flights all by herself without anyone knowing about it." Maile noticed the two girls were flashing eye contact at each other. "Samantha, this is Thérèse, a friend from Maui. Thérèse, this is Samantha, a troublemaker from Iowa."

"Ohio."

"Wherever."

The girls shook hands the way new classmates at school would.

"Are you mad at me?" Samantha asked.

"Of course I am!" Maile saw the girl's reaction and softened her tone. "A little. But we need to call your mother. She must be frantic." She got out her phone and scrolled through numbers. "I don't know if I have your mother's number."

"You can use my phone." Samantha handed hers over, the latest model that even business people lusted after.

"Nice phone."

"It's great. Lots of memory and has superfast data. I even made the...never mind."

"You booked your flights using your phone?" Maile asked.

"Maybe."

"That's a yes or no question, and I think your mother and I deserve to know the answer."

Samantha looked down at the floor. "Yes."

Maile found the mother's number and called, wondering what to say. "Hello, Mrs. Gibson? This is Maile Spencer, in Honolulu. Maybe you remember me as your tour guide a few months ago?"

"Yes, I do. Hello, Maile. I'm very sorry, but something terrible has happened, and I can't talk right now."

"Something about Samantha? Because she's here with me."

"What?" Maile listened as Samantha's mother yelled at others at her end on the call to gather around her, that there was news about Sammy. "What's she doing there? Where are you? Is this a..."

Maile had to interrupt before the call got out of hand. "Samantha is fine. We're in Honolulu, at the airport. I'm here to pick up someone else, and I found your daughter here at the terminal. Apparently, she booked flights to get here and never told you about it."

"She's okay?"

"She's homesick and probably hungry. I'll get her a meal in a few minutes. What do you want me to do?"

After a lengthy explanation to the others with her in Ohio, Mrs. Gibson sighed audibly on the phone. "Put her on."

Maile held the phone aloft for a moment before giving it to Samantha. "She wants to talk to you. Better be nice to her because you're in big trouble."

Maile listened as the girl apologized and started crying again, while she stared down at Thérèse.

"Do you have a phone?"

"Yes."

Maile held her hand out. "Give it to me."

"But…"

"Now."

Thérèse found her phone and put it in Maile's hand, who promptly turned it off and put it in her bag. By then, Samantha was giving her phone back to Maile. "She wants to talk to you again."

"Mrs. Gibson, what do you want me to do with Samantha?"

"I can't say that out loud. We're already making flight reservations to come pick her up. That might not be until later tonight. Is there any way I can talk you into babysitting her?"

It was Maile's turn to sigh. "I already have one girl for the day."

"I'd really appreciate it. Otherwise…"

"Otherwise, I'd have to call the police and they'd get Child Protective Services involved..." Maile made a point of glaring at Samantha. "...and that would cause more trouble than what it's worth. She can stay with me, but I'll need to be reimbursed for all expenses."

After promising to send flight and arrival details to Maile's phone, Mrs. Gibson ended the call. Maile put Samantha's phone in her bag with Thérèse's.

"She didn't want to talk to me again?" Samantha asked with big eyes still wet with tears.

"I think your mom is little too mad to be nice to you right now." Once they were headed to the parking lot, Maile got out her own phone and dialed the number of a friend. "Detective Ota, I have a quick question for you."

"A little busy right now, Maile. Can it wait?"

"Bustin' a perp? Putting the cuffs on my friend, Suzie Suzuki?"

"On a stakeout. In one minute or less, what do you need?" he asked.

"Is it trouble if a kid comes from the mainland to visit me without getting her parents' permission first?"

"How old's the kid?"

"Ten."

"Have you called the parents?"

"Yes. I talked to the mother. She wants me to watch the girl until she gets here later tonight."

"Do you have a witness to that conversation?"

"Only the kid. But I have a record of the call on the phone. Do I need to contact anyone here?"

"Like CPS? Only if you want trouble. Time's up. Gotta go."

Keepers of the Kingdom

Chapter Two

Maile's phone rang as soon as Detective Ota's call was done. It was Lani, the bride, again.

"Almost here?"

Maile could tell her friend was either in tears or near them. "Just tell me what's wrong?"

"Just hurry and get here!"

"Who's that?" Thérèse asked.

"The bride."

"What's she crying about?" Samantha asked.

"People asking her too many questions." Maile put her phone away when they got to her car. The back door creaked when she opened it for the girls to climb in. "Seat belts on, low and tight."

"Just like on the plane?" Samantha asked.

"Exactly like on the plane. Only that you go where I go and nowhere else." Maile said a silent prayer when she turned the ignition key. It was answered when the engine spun to life on the first try. She was quickly on the highway back to town. When Maile looked at what the girls were doing, Thérèse had her lunch sack open and they were dividing up the contents. They each took half a sandwich, one got the juice box, while the other got the fruit bowl. They saved the carrot sticks for last.

"Maile, what's half of five?"

"One-fourth of ten."

"We don't have ten carrot sticks."

"You guys are old enough to figure out fractions. It's just like at school. This is real life practical use of fractions."

Maile did her best not to chuckle while the girls, really just strangers to each other, as they determined the answer counting on fingers and writing in the air.

"That's two and a half sticks each. We don't have a knife to cut one in half."

"Thanks goodness. You'll have to break it."

Again, she watched as they negotiated who got the larger half.

"Sammy, Thérèse and I already have our day planned out. Since you broke a lot of rules to come here, you don't get much choice about what we do today."

"But…"

"Sorry."

"It's okay if she gets a vote," Thérèse said quietly.

"We'll see about that."

"Maybe we can vote to see if she gets a vote?"

Maile gave the clever idea some thought. "Only if I retain veto power. You know what that is?"

"Yeah, you get to cancel our votes."

"You know why?" Maile asked.

"Cuz you're bigger than us?" Samantha said.

"Very good. But right now, we have a wedding to go to."

Samantha instantly brightened. "Wedding? Yours?"

"Fortunately, no. It's a rehearsal for a real wedding tomorrow, and I'm in it."

"Gonna wear a pretty dress?"

"Of course."

"Can we come to the wedding?" Thérèse asked. "Never been to a wedding on Oahu before."

"I've never been to a wedding in Hawaii before," Samantha said.

"Bride in a white gown, groom in a tuxedo, and a minister in a church. Not much different from anywhere else. Just more flowers." Maile parked in front of the old church in the center of the city. "Later this evening, you'll both be back with your mothers again, and I bet Sammy will be on her way home by tomorrow morning. Both of you will be home in time for Thanksgiving dinner next week."

The girls had to trot to keep up with Maile when she went in through the front door of the church. Most of the wedding party had assembled near the altar at the front, while Lani was off to one side, surrounded by her mother and the other bridesmaids. Ronald was there, talking to the minister, looking worried about something. With a second scan of the church occupants, Maile couldn't tell what was upsetting Lani so much. Putting her hands on the shoulders of both girls, she pushed them down into the last pew.

"If either one of you makes a move, you're both in trouble. Understand?"

"Big trouble?" Samantha asked.

"Colossal trouble."

Getting nods from both of them, Maile went to see Lani. She couldn't tell if the dramatics were just ending or beginning, but it wasn't pretty. "What's going on?"

"Look," Lisa, the maid of honor, said. "Look behind the altar."

Confused with the command, Maile looked at the back wall of the church. It took a moment before she noticed something was missing. Two things. "Where're the kahili?"

"That's what we want to know," Lisa said.

"They were missing when we got here this morning," another bridesmaid said. It was Lei-lei, one of Maile's oldest and dearest friends, an old nursing school classmate and workmate at the hospital.

"Did you talk to Reverend Akamu? Does he know anything about where they might be?"

They were all seated in a pew together now. "He's as surprised as the rest of us," Lani's mother said.

"All my life, I've looked at those kahili, knowing they'd be there during my wedding," Lani said. "I know it's silly, but as a little kid, I thought they represented the bride and groom that would say I do to each other. A touch of royalty for a commoner's wedding, you know? Now they're not there and no one seems to know where they went."

Feeling compelled to do something, Maile went to Reverend Akamu for a few answers.

"It's a mystery to all of us, Maile," he told her. "Maybe we should hold the rehearsal now. Once that's done, I can make a few phone calls to see if anyone knows where they might be."

She walked with him to the front of the church. "When was the last time you saw them, Reverend?"

"I saw both yesterday afternoon. I'll have to call the custodian. Maybe he noticed them last evening when he closed up and locked the doors."

"Who's taking care of the place these days?"

"Young man. Fred something. Haole from the mainland. I usually don't handle those matters, the office staff does. He seemed down and out, and needed a job. Maybe I found the wrong man to help?"

"Or he found you." It was odd, that someone from the mainland would be given a job taking care of a Hawaiian church that had been used by royalty in the past, now considered Hawaii's Westminster Abbey. It was the oldest church in Honolulu, and still held weekly congregations to anyone who wanted to visit and worship with the others. It also held special events like christenings and baptisms, and was especially popular with people from all over the world for weddings. As a little girl, Maile had fantasized about getting married there, but her wedding was held at the much smaller and humbler family church near her home. "That's very kind of you to give him a job."

The group went through a quick walk-through of the ceremony, going right up to the moment when the bride and groom would trade 'I dos'. While the other bridesmaids chatted afterward, Maile found Brock Turner, sergeant with the Honolulu Police Department. He was one of the groomsmen, opposite in position from Maile. Even though it was a day off for him and he was in civvies, he was making notes in the ever-present little notepad all police officers carried.

"Is this something the police get involved in?" she asked.

"Missing church property? You bet. I'm already taking notes for a report I'll file later. Do you happen to have any recent pictures of the kahili?"

"Not me. There should be plenty of pictures online. They change the color of the fabric every now and then, though."

"That's what I thought. Any idea of the most recent colors?"

"Red and yellow of the House of Kamehameha. The pole is about six feet high altogether, with only the top half decorated. These kahili in the church have more modern styling, with red and yellow feathers at the upper part, and red velvet fabric below, with is gathered around the pole mid-way down."

"The fabric is red?"

"Deep red velvet. It's bunched together with a yellow cord of some sort."

"Most of the upper part was red, and the top and bottom were yellow, right?" he asked, still taking notes.

Maile tried not to laugh. Subjects like kahili and the feathered cloaks of the ali'i were taught to schoolchildren all over Hawaii, and it was something anybody who identified as being even part Hawaiian took pride in. Brock was one-eighth Hawaiian and should know, in Maile's view. "Brah, this is your heritage. Don't you know about these things?"

"Apparently, not as well as you do. Is there an easy answer, or are you going to make me work for it?"

"Since you don't know, I might make you suffer a little. Red and yellow are the colors of Hawaiian royalty, especially that of the House of Kamehameha. Each monarch had their own color, and Queen Lili'uokalani favored green. In fact, I've seen watercolor prints of the kahili of when she was still the reigning monarch, and they would've been green and black when she came to visit the church. Along with the usual red and yellow, of course."

"Of course. Didn't she attend Saint Andrew's Cathedral?" Brock asked.

"Later on. She grew up here in Kawaiaha'o, and often played the organ and led the choir here. I imagine she was a member of both congregations."

He flipped his notepad closed and tucked it away in a pocket. "I'll take a look at the cathedral to see if the kahili might've shown up there, and then file a report downtown."

"Ask if they might loan out a pair of their kahili for tomorrow's wedding."

"They're that important?" he asked.

"Lani's pretty upset. Women plan their weddings from before they can spell the word. We're not happy unless everything's perfect. I get the idea that those missing kahili are as important to her as any of the flowers that'll decorate this place tomorrow. This is the big event of the year, and we all want it to turn out perfect. Other than wilted flowers, I can't imagine anything bigger than this going wrong."

"I'll look into it." He shifted nervously. "Are you busy the rest of the day? There's something we need to talk about."

Maile nodded at her two charges, still seated in the last pew. They'd stopped whispering, now looking pensive about something, the way only little girls can.

"Playing mommy today."

"You've taken up babysitting?"

"Look again. That's very high-class babysitting duty. The one with dark hair is the daughter of Maui's mayor."

"I thought she looked familiar. Who's the other kid?" he asked.

"Might be best if I didn't tell you."

"Why?"

"Something of a runaway, all the way from Ohio. She and her family were here on vacation a few months ago and she decided to come back without telling anyone about it."

"Somebody's coming to claim her?" he asked.

"Claim her? She's not lost luggage, brah. But yeah, her mother is coming in later tonight."

While talking with Brock, Maile kept an eye on her two young charges. They seemed to be getting along well, even whispering secrets to each other from time to time. When Maile finally joined up with them again, she could tell they were ready to go.

"Can we go to the restroom?" Samantha begged.

"Oh, that's why the two of you look so worried."

After she sent the kids on their way, she found Lei-lei just leaving.

"As if there's already not enough stress, Lani freaks out over the kahili," Lei-lei said. "I could use a cigarette."

"I thought you quit?"

"I did, for several months now. But this wedding is turning into a production. Those kahili being lost aren't helping anything."

"I get the feeling Lani's crying over more than just the kahili," Maile said.

"What're we supposed to do now?"

"I'm looking for the kahili. That much I can fix. Whatever else is going on is on them. Then this evening, we have the party. At noon tomorrow, Lani gets married. By three o'clock, she and Ronald will be on their honeymoon and my face will be numb from one glass of champagne too many."

"Who are the kids following you around?" Lei-lei asked.

"Strays." Maile saw the girls coming back. "Long story. I'll tell you later."

Wondering if a fresh pack of cigarettes was in her friend's near future, Maile took the girls to her car.

"Who's the guy?" Samantha asked once her seatbelt was buckled.

"What guy?"

"The guy you were talking to for so long," Thérèse said.

"Brock. Sergeant Brock Turner, of the Honolulu Police Department."

"Oh," said Samantha quietly. "He's taking me to jail?"

"Maybe. Worried about something?"

"I don't want to go to jail, if that's what you're gonna do with me."

Maile looked at both of them in her rearview mirror. She had some leverage and planned to use it. "You won't go to jail if you don't get in trouble. And if either one of you gets in trouble, both of you go to jail. Understand?"

"Yes," the girls said in unison.

"Can we get lunch now?" one asked.

"How can you be hungry?" Maile asked as she weaved through traffic in streets that she'd known all her life. "You just ate Thérèse's lunch."

"Kinda like starved," Samantha said.

"I could eat something," Thérèse said. "You guys have any vegetarian restaurants around here?"

"Not specifically that I know of, but I know a place that…" Maile's phone rang. She checked the number. Being one she figured she should take, she pulled into a gas station and stopped. "Detective Ota. How are you? I thought you were busy right now?"

"Not so great. Where are you? Do you have time to meet?"

"Just trying to decide on what to have for lunch."

"Good. Come to Chop Suey City. Remember where it's at?"

"How could I not? I've been there with you and your police buddies often enough." She saw the girls chatting again in the back seat. "Hey, do you know if they have vegetarian meals there?"

"I don't know. Just show up."

Wondering why Ota was more testy than usual, Maile aimed for the strip mall Chinese restaurant in the middle of town.

Maile glanced at the girls in the back seat. "You guys like Chinese food?"

The girls looked at each other for the answer and answered together. "I guess."

"Not much of an answer, but that's what we're having for lunch." When she parked, she got the kids together for a powwow. "Okay, I'm having a lot of fun with you guys so far, but it's still early."

"We'll be good," Samantha promised. Thérèse nodded her head in agreement.

"I have an idea. Let's start a club."

The girls' faces brightened. "What's it called?"

"How about the Keepers of the Kingdom?"

"Us too?" Samantha asked.

"All three of us." Maile took her umbrella from her bag and stretched it out without opening it. "I, Princess Hokuhoku'ikalani, pronounce you Thérèse, daughter of Melanie the ali'i of Maui, and Sammy, daughter of the Royal Gibsons of Ohio, official Keepers of the Kingdom."

She ceremoniously tapped them on the shoulders with her umbrella.

"Just don't forget I'm in charge."

Chapter Three

Maile led the girls into the restaurant that was ornately decorated with what she considered modern kitsch. Even though she liked Chinese food, she had a distaste for this particular place. They were met by the same waitress as always, a tall Chinese girl dressed in a red cheongsam.

Maile's sense of jealousy acted up, the girl being something of a rival in her quest for romance with a mutual man of interest. Her suntanned skin, unstyled hair, and athletic runner's body just couldn't compete with the waitress's pearlescent complexion, glossy hair, or softly feminine figure. Those were only the beginning of Maile's problems with the waitress.

"Three of us today, Miss Wong."

Acting as if she was expecting Maile, the waitress led them to a large table in a back corner where Detective Ota was waiting.

What Maile didn't expect to find were half a dozen other police officers in uniforms, all eating a group lunch. Brock Turner was there right in the middle of them, and she wasn't sure if she was happy about that or not. He was the 'person of interest' that held the attention of both Maile and Miss Wong.

The girls edged behind her when Maile stopped at the table. Two of the officers pulled out chairs for them while the others made space between them.

"Quiet day of crime on the streets of Honolulu?" Maile asked, after all the introductions were done.

"Ms. Spencer, sit with me," Ota said, setting his menu down.

Maile watched carefully as the girls split up and sat between officers across the round table from her. When the waitress handed them menus, Maile asked, "Is there a kid's menu?"

"We have a kid's combo A meal, and a kid's combo B meal."

"What's the difference?"

"Not much."

"Bring them one of each, and I'll have the regular combo B with rice and pork." She tried not to notice when most of the men at the table watched as the waitress walked away, taking her hips and hair with her. "Guys, let me introduce my friends. This is Thérèse from Maui, and Samantha visiting from Iowa."

"Ohio," Samantha said shyly.

"Sorry. I'm sure they're both nice."

She let the cops do their own introductions, since she didn't recognize half of them. Detective Ota's meal came, another combination plate, and gave it some scrutiny. Its savory scent made her realize how hungry she was. In a blink of an eye, the kids' lunches were brought out. One had a scoop of fried rice, mixed vegetables, and French fries, and the other had the same but Tater Tots instead of the fries. She watched as the girls negotiated swaps in foods, vegetarian Thérèse trading away her pork fried rice for Samantha's Tots, while Samantha looked happy to get the rice. That required the assistance of the officers at the table, who made something of a game of passing things back and forth. On the heels of their meals came her own combo plate, steaming hot with the scent of garlic.

"Okay, what's so important that we need to meet half of Honolulu's finest for lunch?" she asked Ota.

"Your friend, Prince Aziz, is out."

"Not my friend and why is he out? He's on trial for human trafficking, elicitation of prostitution, and being weird. Some of them are federal offenses, even international, which is why he's being tried in federal court. Why is he walking free?"

"First of all, being weird isn't a crime. If it was, half of us would be in prison, and the other half would be hiding," Ota said.

"I bet that Mrs. Abrams dropped the charges against him, didn't she?"

"Not exactly. The judge tossed the case out, implying Abrams didn't have enough evidence. He's giving her a few weeks to get her stuff together before she can refile for a new trial."

"What? Why'd he do that?" she asked.

"Abrams' star witness pulled out, citing she wanted nothing to do with the case. That witness is you, Ms. Spencer."

"Oh." She knew Ota was mad at her because he was back to calling her 'Ms. Spencer' instead of by her first name. She noticed that their conversation had caught the attention of the others at the table, who were listening intently. "But if all she has on Aziz is my witness testimony, she doesn't have much of a case, right? Is that why the judge threw it out?"

"Exactly why."

"And now, I'm sure she's blaming me?"

"Probably. All she has as evidence is your statement to the police, which was me, the night he solicited you. She doesn't need you in court as a witness, but that statement you gave back then is only good enough to show intent to solicit a prostitute, and since you don't work the streets, there's only intent to solicit..." He looked at the two girls at the table listening to him. "...bedroom activities, as it were."

Miss Wong had come back to the table. Maile watched very carefully as the pretty waitress lingered a little too long and way too closely at Brock's side before taking away his plate. She didn't hear what was said in their friendly dialogue. After some internal cursing, she went back to the conversation with Detective Ota.

"The Prince gave me money, a lot of it, and promised more if I'd spend the night with him. You and those FBI agents saw it that evening. Isn't that prostitution?"

"Aziz adamantly denies it was meant for that, and was simply a tip for a good tour you gave him earlier that day. Either way, that makes it only be a local jurisdiction matter, not something for federal courts. And if I were to bring him in on charges of prostitution, I'd have to bring in you also, Ms. Spencer. Can't have solicitation without a girl, or whoever, that would've provided the service. Not to mention starting a diplomatic nightmare that would stretch from here to Washington DC."

"Where is he now?" she asked.

"Still on Oahu. He still can't leave the island until Abrams or a judge says he can."

Maile had lost most of her appetite for her combination plate. "Abrams has sent you to work on me? Is that all this is about?"

"No. I just came to warn you that he's out there somewhere."

"So what do I care?"

"You care because he might not be happy about having to share the island with you."

"I'm not going to hide under my kitchen table, Detective Ota, just because some lame prince from Nowhereland is holding a grudge." The waitress was able to sneak in the check for the meal as she took Maile's plate away. On it were the kids' meals also. "I have a life to live."

"There's something else."

"Seriously tired of hearing about the Prince," she said, putting down enough cash to pay for the meals, but not enough for a tip. The Prince wasn't the only one that could hold a grudge. If Miss Wong was going to hang that close to something Maile had her eye on, she wasn't going to be rewarded for it.

"It isn't about the Prince. This is about someone else. First, let me ask if you've visited Honolulu Med lately? More precisely, any time yesterday?"

"You told me to stay away from there, even though half my friends work there, and I have. Why do you ask that?"

"Your other friend, Oscar Swenberg, has disappeared from his hospital bed."

"Maybe he was discharged?" she asked. Swenberg had been another source of trouble for Maile, even up to a few days before.

"The hospital is the one who called us about a missing patient. We have to treat it as a missing person case, since he would be considered vulnerable being a hospital patient."

"He might've left AMA."

"Which is?" he asked.

"Against Medical Advice. He would've checked himself out by walking out the front door. Generally considered a bad idea."

"Somehow, he left without a trace and when no one was looking."

"Let me guess. You have his house and yacht staked out and he hasn't shown up?"

"You don't know where he might be?" Ota asked.

"Not a clue. I have as much interest in Oscar Swenberg as I do in the Prince of Nowhereland."

"Been in touch with Laurie Long?" Ota asked.

"Is that what Honey's going by again? The last I heard, she was still Honey Humdinger."

"You don't like her much, do you?"

"Biggest fraud in town," she said.

"Why?"

"Local girl sophistication with a Hollywood façade." Most of the cops had gone back on patrol by then, leaving only Brock behind. He was busy entertaining her charges with magic tricks. "Girls, are you ready to go?"

"Go to where?" Samantha asked.

"While the police look for missing criminals, the three of us are going to look for the missing kahili. That should be fun, right?"

Maile was quick to get the girls out to the parking lot, wondering if her car was going to start again. Before they could climb in, Brock caught up with them.

"I'm on my way to check with the people at Saint Andrew's right now about the kahili," he said. "Do you know anybody there?"

She shook her head. "Just the people at our little congregation in Manoa, and a few at Kawaiaha'o. Reverend Akamu didn't seem to know anything about the kahili. I'll check with Reverend Ka'uhane at the Manoa church, but I doubt he'll know anything. Any leads or ideas for where to look for them?"

"I have no idea," he said.

"Doesn't help much."

"Start at the beginning. Figure out who has the most to gain by stealing the kahili. That's assuming they were stolen. They might be out being cleaned or conserved. I checked with Reverend Akamu and he has a busy schedule of weddings in the next few weeks. Maybe they're getting cleaned ahead of time? Or somebody decided to swap them out for something else?"

"Maybe." She noticed the girls looking bored. "I'm not spending a whole lot of time on my little investigation, though. I need to find something for them to do. Once I have them dropped off with their mothers, care to go out this evening?"

"Like a date?" he asked. He shifted his weight from one foot to the other.

"Yeah, like a date. You, me, dark restaurant, footsies under the table. Since we're supposed to be a pretend couple tomorrow for the wedding as groomsman and bridesmaid, I thought we could kick things off tonight?"

"You see…" He glanced back at the restaurant. "I already have something planned."

"Oh, with…that waitress?"

"Her name is Mei Ling."

Maile got in her car, slammed the door shut, jammed the key in the ignition, and put the window down. "Have fun on your date with Mail Order Mei Ling."

"That almost sounds…"

"Like jealousy?"

"Racist."

Maile was embarrassed, knowing it sounded that way. To her, it was pure jealousy. "My apologies to the human race."

"For?"

"Being human." Maile said a silent prayer before turning the key. It didn't start this time. She popped the hood and looked beneath.

"Need a hand?"

"Why don't you…"

"Do what?" a different man asked.

"Oh, it's you," Maile said to Detective Ota. He was next to her, watching her twist wires and slap grimy parts. "Where's a lawyer when you need one?"

"You're going to sue your car?"

"Have it committed. I thought you were done lecturing me for the day?"

"Not going to lecture you." He opened the trunk of his car and got a crate of avocados for her. "Where do you want these?"

"I'm supposed to eat all those?"

"In time. These are the last few from my tree. I'd rather give them to someone than fill the yard waste bin."

"I'm so lucky. I didn't know you were a gardener. Actually, I didn't know you ever went home from work."

"They're getting heavy," he said.

Maile knew better than to risk her expensive new nails on a crate of fruit. As it was, she already had engine grime under a few of them. She opened the trunk of her car and made space. "Girls, help the detective."

Thérèse and Samantha shared the load of putting the crate in the car.

"You're a real detective?" Samantha asked.

"I am." Ota looked down at the girl and smiled. "Are you a real girl?"

"Huh?"

"He's teasing you, Sammy," Maile said.

"Can we eat some of the avocados?" Thérèse asked.

"I don't know. Do you have teeth?"

Thérèse winced at the question. "Are you sure you're a real detective?"

With that, Maile got the kids loaded into the car. The engine started on the first try.

"Hey, you got your car fixed," Brock said, stepping back to watch smoke come from the exhaust pipe. He'd been watching the exchange of fruit.

"Yeah, David fixed it for me this morning. You know the lawyer David Melendez, right?"

"Yes, but how'd…"

Maile waved at Brock as she backed out of the parking space. "Sorry! Gotta go! Have a case to solve!"

Once they were in traffic, the girls got active in the back seat.

"You like that guy, huh?" Samantha asked.

"Yeah. A little, maybe."

"Shoulda kissed him," Thérèse said.

"What? Why?"

"Because you like him!" Samantha said.

"I think he's interested in someone else right now."

"That waitress?" Thérèse asked.

"Oh, you noticed too?"

"Of course we did," Samantha said.

"Gotta be blind not to notice that," Thérèse said.

Maile wasn't sure why she was discussing her bruised heart that resulted in failing to get a date for that evening with a couple of ten-year-olds. "I can't compete with someone who looks like her."

"I think that guy liked her dress," Samantha said.

"More to what he likes about her than the dress," Maile muttered. She turned the steering wheel hard to make a lane change, resulting in getting honked at.

"That's why you shoulda kissed him," Thérèse said.

"Like you guys are experts in romance?"

"I've seen all the movies," Samantha said.

"There's a lot more to romance than what you see in the movies."

"Why?"

"I don't know," Maile said, narrowly missing bumping a curb as she made a turn. "It's very complicated."

"When my mom kisses the fire chief, he likes it," Thérèse said. "I bet that guy would like it if you kissed him."

"Can we talk about something else besides my love life, please?"

"Is there something more fun to talk about than kissing boys?" Samantha asked.

"Yes, the missing kahili. Any big ideas of who might've stole it?"

"Are they really that important for a wedding?" Samantha asked.

"Just Hawaiian stuff, right?" Thérèse asked.

"Well, the kahili are part of Hawaiian history, and the bride is part Hawaiian. Lani has been planning this wedding all her life, and I guess those kahili were always a part of her idea of the perfect wedding. It'd be too bad if she didn't have them."

"Important stuff," Thérèse said.

"Are we supposed to plan our weddings?" Samantha asked.

"You'll start thinking about it pretty soon." Maile parked in the lot at the church she normally went to when she had time on Sundays. There was only one other car in the lot, that of Reverend Ka'uhane, and she tapped bumpers with it just as she stopped.

"Not a very good driver, huh?" Thérèse said as they got out of the car.

"What makes you think that?"

"Always bumping into stuff."

"Am not."

"Four times already," Samantha said.

"You're counting?"

"Four times…so far," Thérèse said. Then speaking as if she'd learned a few diplomacy tactics from her mother, added, "That's okay. My auntie bumps into stuff all the time. She's not so good either."

Maile held the door open for the kids to go in. "Can we focus on why we're here, please?"

"Why are we at another church, anyway?" Thérèse asked.

"Yeah. Do you go to church every day, or something?" Samantha added.

"If I knew of a convent in town, I'd drop the two of you off there," Maile said.

"Huh?" the girls said in unison.

"Starting our search for the kahili, remember?" Maile said. "I'm hoping Reverend Ka'uhane might know something about them. Maybe you guys should wait here in the chapel while I talk to him. Can you do that without wandering off?"

They nodded in unison.

"Okay, so, no playing, no noise, and please don't break anything."

"Been in churches before," one of them said as they went off on a self-guided tour of the building.

"Something's going wrong," Maile muttered as she went to Reverend Ka'uhane's office. "I just know it."

She was invited in and took a seat in the elderly minister's office. His eyes still had a twinkle to them, and his smile was as crooked as ever. His shoulders were hunched and his hair had gone white since she'd listened to his sermons as a child, but he was still the same kindly man she'd known all her life.

"Not so much trouble on your face these days, Maile."

She sat with her bag on her lap. "Maybe not. My divorce is final. I'm not sure if that's good or not."

"Are you happier without him?"

"Mostly. I get a little lonely sometimes."

"Some of the best marriages have a husband or wife that feel lonely occasionally. Some of the worst marriages are filled with busy people. Is that why you're here today?"

"No, actually, there's a little trouble at Kawaiaha'o Church."

"I just got off a call from my old friend Akamu. The kahili have disappeared from behind the altar?"

Maile nodded. "A friend of mine is having her wedding there tomorrow, and is upset. I'm spending today looking for them. Kinda silly, I guess."

"Are the police involved?" he asked.

"They've taken a report. But you know them. They're busy investigating bigger crimes than missing kahili."

"And that's why you're involved?"

"Right. I just want Lani to have the wedding she's always dreamed of."

He sat quietly for a moment. "It's interesting that you've taken up this task of making a perfect wedding for your friend on the heels of your own divorce."

"That's been troubling me all day, too. Is there something wrong with that?"

"You need to ask yourself that question." Reverend Ka'uhane adjusted his position in his chair. "Maile, I think it's very warm-hearted of you to make sure your friend has the wedding of her dreams. Every bride deserves that. But are you trying to make up for the loss you're feeling over your own marriage by focusing on the details of her wedding?"

"Maybe it's a little of that. I feel bad for Lani, but I feel even worse that something from our Hawaiian heritage is missing from where it belongs."

"Certainly not the first time something has been taken from us. Why are the kahili so important?" he asked.

"Queen Lili'uokalani would've seen them when she attended services a century ago, maybe even handled them."

"You're not making this more important than what it really is?" Reverend Ka'uhane asked. "They're just kahili, after all."

"Yep, just koa wood poles polished by hands and time, and rare feathers collected from birds long extinct, and used as royal standards by Hawaiian ali'i. Nothing important at all."

"You know what I mean," he said. "That's how the police are looking at them, and maybe we should, too."

"We have so few things like that, that we need to do whatever we can to preserve them. I guess the idea of someone not worthy of handling them, or even worse, selling them for a few bucks, makes me sick."

"Then go look for the kahili, not for your friend's wedding, but for the sake of our heritage. You'll have more strength and stamina in that quest than for any other reason." Reverend Ka'uhane smiled. "Who are your little friends that came with you today?"

"Thérèse and Samantha. I'm something of a glorified babysitter for Thérèse until her mother gets here from Maui later today, and Samantha found her way onto a flight from Ohio, all by herself without telling anyone."

45

"Clever little girl."

"Both of them are. And handfuls. Speaking of which, I better go find them before something gets dismantled." Looking in her bag, she got the three avocados she brought for him.

He took one in a hand. "I've never seen an avocado tree at your mother's house."

"I got a crate of them from a friend. The problem is that we're not avocado eaters."

Reverend Ka'uhane ended their visit with a short prayer in Hawaiian. When Maile returned to the chapel, neither of the girls were around. "Now what are they up to?"

Chapter Four

Maile looked up and down every pew to see if maybe the girls were playing hide and seek before going outside. There wasn't much to the property, just a lawn with a few hibiscus and ti plants near the doors, and a small parking lot. Otherwise, there was an attached building with two rooms for Sunday School classes, a community room, and a small kitchen. When she saw the back door to the kitchen propped open, she hurried there. That's where she found both of them eating sandwiches.

"Oh, here you are. Why are you eating again? We just had lunch a little while ago."

"That was Chinese food," Maile's mother said. Kealoha was at the sink cutting stems and making flower arrangements for the weekend meetings and services. Maile also spotted two other sandwiches on the counter, something that her mother had made for her and Reverend Ka'uhane to share later. "Both so skinny. They need more than that."

Maile looked at the sandwich in Thérèse's hand. "Is that vegetarian?"

The girl nodded. "Peanut butter and lettuce."

"Lettuce?"

"It's what she asked for," Kealoha said.

"I have bacon, lettuce and tomato, without the bacon," Samantha said. "I'm going to be a vegetarian, too."

"When you're done eating, we have places to go."

"Where?" they asked in unison.

"First, the Bishop Museum to talk to the curator of the kahili room."

"I heard about the kahili that are missing from the Kawaiaha'o Church. Even the police are involved in a big investigation?" Kealoha asked.

"Where'd you hear that?" Maile asked.

"Your two friends told me all about it."

"Not so much of an investigation. Only a report and a shrug."

"But they said you met with several police officers?" Kealoha said.

Maile made half a BLT sandwich of her own, also without the bacon. "That was at lunch. I seriously doubt they're looking very hard for a couple of sticks with feathers and velvet on them."

"Don't make fun of them. They're very important," Maile's mother said.

"To us, and to the people who go to church at Kawaiaha'o, but pretty low priority to the police. That's why I'm spending the day looking for them. Even if it's just asking around the community if anyone might know where they went, it's better than nothing."

"What about your little friends?" Kealoha asked. "Aren't you supposed to be entertaining them instead of taking them on your hunt?"

"Thérèse is up for anything, right, Thérèse?" The girl nodded her agreement while chewing her mouthful of sandwich. Maile pretended to glare at Samantha. "And Sammy is in the doghouse. She doesn't get to vote on what we do or where we go. She's just along for the ride until her mother gets here."

"Has she been trouble to you?" Kealoha asked.

"Well, no, but…"

"Does Thérèse mind that Sammy's joined you?"

"Okay with me," Thérèse said, after gulping milk.

"Then include her in the group, and let her mother decide what's best for Sammy when she gets here. No need to make the little one suffer more than necessary. She said she came here to hang around with you, after all. Let her have some fun."

"I guess."

"Dark clouds are coming in her direction soon enough," Kealoha said, taking empty plates and glasses to the sink.

Samantha propped her face on a hand. "Yeah, dark clouds and grounded for like forever."

"Didn't think about that before you made the flight reservations, did you?" Maile asked, finishing her own glass of milk.

"Oh, leave the girl alone," Kealoha said. "You had your fair share of being grounded when you were her age."

"Never ran away from home on an airplane." Maile had the girls use the restroom before they went out to the car. "Next stop, Bishop Museum."

"What's there?" Samantha asked.

"Old stuff," Thérèse said before Maile could answer.

"Cool place," Maile said. "Part natural history, part culture, part art exhibit. We can learn a lot about the history of Hawaii there. They also have a kahili room, a space set aside specifically for the remaining kahili of the ali'i and monarchs of Hawaii. Very interesting."

"Don't get to touch stuff," Thérèse said.

"That's how museums usually work. Sounds like you've been there before?" Maile asked. Once again, as if her prayers were answered, her car started.

"Chance and me got in trouble the last time. My mom had to make all kinds of promises stuff wouldn't happen again." Maile noticed in the rearview mirror Thérèse wincing from some sort of internal strife. "I think she made a big donation."

"And that made them happy?"

Thérèse's wince grew even more. "It made them shut up."

"Okay, I don't know what happened, but we'll leave that in the past. I remember they have garden activities outside for kids. I think it might be best if you guys do that while I talk to a conservator about the kahili."

It took only a few minutes to get to the popular museum. It always struck Maile how out of place the old stone building and green lawns looked situated in the middle of a commercial and light industrial part of the city. Checking the girls in for an hour-long day camp on how to grow tropical plants that have healing properties, she took them aside.

"Okay, you're signed in for an hour. They have people here to help you, but it's mostly unsupervised. Do you know what that means?"

This time, the girls rolled their eyes in unison. "It means don't break stuff," Thérèse said, with Samantha nodding her agreement.

"It also means don't wander off."

"Why would we do that?" Samantha asked.

"Oh, I don't know. Maybe if you saw something shiny, you might chase after it. Or maybe, just to be naughty, you might get on a plane and fly around the world."

"Not goin' anywhere," Samantha said. "Jeesh. You sound just like my mom."

Maile left them to the fates and headed off to the museum's entrance. "Speaking of which, I need to give Mrs. Gibson a call to see when to pick her up at the airport. I wouldn't mind if Doctor Kato got here a little early, also."

Waiting in the shade just outside the main entrance, she called Samantha's mother.

"Good news! I'm packed and ready to go to the airport."

"What? You're still in Ohio?"

"Yes, sorry about the delay."

"Were there flight connection problems?" Maile asked.

"The flight from California to Hawaii was easy. Even getting a flight from Ohio to California wasn't so bad. It's just getting from our little town to the airport in the city that's been the hard part."

"No one could give you a ride?"

"No one had the time to give me a ride all the way into Cleveland, so I have to fly from Columbus. Not so many connections from there. It ended up being more expensive to fly from Columbus than if I'd taken the bus to Cleveland. Could've taken an earlier flight, too. I'm not much of a tour agent."

The woman's kid was five thousand miles away staying with a stranger, and she was worried about the cost of a plane ticket. "Don't worry about it. What time do you get in?"

"First thing tomorrow morning. They call it a redeye flight..."

"Tomorrow?" Maile's attitude sank as quickly as her shoulders drooped. "Okay, text me the flight details and I'll pick you up when you get in."

"Do you have a place for Sammy to sleep? Because if you need to get a room, you can charge it to my credit card..."

Maile made a point of sighing audibly. "I have someplace for her to stay that won't be expensive. But I have a wedding to attend at noon, and need to be at the church an hour before. I'll need an hour to get ready, and want to spend some time with the bride. You know, all those usual bridesmaid things that we like to do, such as having breakfast together, and it won't be easy if I have a kid with me."

Mrs. Gibson's voice lowered. "I'm very sorry, Maile. I've put you in an awkward spot. I forgot that you have a life of your own, and you've taken up the task of being Sammy's tour guide and babysitter."

Now Maile felt bad for scolding the woman. "Sammy's very sweet. We're having fun, but tomorrow is supposed to be about my friend Lani and her wedding, and not about a runaway from...wherever."

After the call, Maile flashed her tour guide ID that got her into museums and exhibits free.

She went straight to the kahili room. At first glance, she could tell the kahili from the church weren't there. No visitors were there at the time, but she found a docent examining one of the exhibits while glancing at a small card in her hand. Maile didn't recognize her from other tour visits, and with the crib notes card in her hand, figured she was new.

"And to think there used to be hundreds of kahili in the islands, and now these are the few that are left," Maile said to get the docent's attention. Her nametag said Estelle Nakajima, a common Japanese family name in the islands, but she looked more Filipino, also common in Hawaii.

Estelle tried hiding an embarrassed smile as she tucked her note card in a pocket. "Yes, not so many these days. Are you here on a tour?"

"No, actually I'm a tour guide visiting on a day off. I was hoping to talk with one of the Kahili Room conservators. Do you know if they're around right now?"

"Do you have an appointment with someone?"

"No, more of a spur of the moment thing. Semi-emergency, I suppose you could call it."

"You'd have to make an appointment. Margaret is busy today with a new acquisition," Estelle said. "I guess that's what I'm supposed to call her. I'm still a little confused about that."

"Margaret Kahele?"

"Yes. You know her?"

"Only in passing. I think we go to the same church," Maile said. Margaret was half a generation older than Maile, and had been in college when Maile was still a girl. She had been known as one of the 'smart people' in the congregation, that if someone had a question about science or history, she was the one to ask. Even though it had been a while since Maile had seen her there, she still attended church services on holidays and special events, about as often as Maile was able to go lately with her schedule as tour guide. "Are you new here, Estelle?"

"Yes, I just graduated university with an art history degree and got a job here. I'm still in docent training."

"You studied kahili in college?" Maile scanned Estelle's face again, looking for any telltale signs of Polynesian heritage and still couldn't find any. "Or native Hawaiian culture and art?"

The docent acted embarrassed again. "Um, no. East Asian art. Mostly Chinese and Japanese ceramics. When I applied for a job here, I thought they'd have me selling tickets. Instead, they stuck…put me in here as the Kahili Room docent." Estelle took the crib notes card from her pocket again. "I don't know anything about these things. I mean, they're very interesting, but what do I know about Hawaiian antiques? I can write a fifty-page paper on a broken tea cup, but I'm lost in this room."

"Well, I don't know anything about ceramics, but I bet your papers on them would be interesting to read." Maile took pity on the girl. Not even asking permission to do so, she launched into a short primer on feathered kahili standards of island ali'i. "In the earliest use of these, the ali'i would use the leg bones of other ali'i they had conquered in battle as the staff, and take the feathers from the conquered's cape to decorate it."

Estelle looked somewhere between appalled and shocked. "That's pretty gruesome."

"That was hundreds of years ago, when much of the world was still waging battle with bows and arrows and spears. I've always wondered if the stories are true about castle knights in Europe pouring boiling oil on invaders as they tried climbing castle walls, or if that's just a Hollywood invention?"

"War isn't much better these days," Estelle said. "Just more efficient."

"Sure seems like it. Anyway, after the conquered ali'i's body had been burnt in a funeral pyre, the longest leg bones were collected, making for one last insult to that village or island ali'i."

"If he couldn't be buried with all his bones, it was like sacrilege?" Estelle asked.

"Exactly. And then to decorate them with feathers and sinew made it even worse. Maybe so many of those battles could've been avoided if they hadn't acted that way. In later years, koa wood staffs were used. That's what most of these are in the museum."

"I've always wondered why they used feathers? That's something I get asked from every tour group that comes through."

"Good question, and there are some interesting answers. There wasn't much back then in the islands to use, just rocks, sand, seawater, plants and flowers, and the few animals that were here. Leaves and flowers are pretty, but don't last long. But there were plenty of birds with colorful feathers, and those lasted a very long time. Look at some of these kahili. Some of them have feathers on them that pre-date the Hawaiian monarchy." They went for a slow walk through the room. "They're still colorful. You can still see the red and yellow colors on some of them."

Estelle referred to her cheat sheet. "I've been learning the different colors of the ali'i. The Kamehameha family used red and yellow, right?"

"Right. And nobody else was allowed to use those colors. There are stories that battles were fought simply because one ali'i tried using the same color feathers as another ali'i. These kahili were like flags. They just couldn't steal someone else's flag without causing trouble."

"Green was for the Kalakaua family?" Estelle asked.

"You got it. And not just any green, or red and yellow. Feathers were collected from very specific birds, just to maintain consistency. It's sad, though. Some of those birds were hunted into extinction, just for the feathers. Now they're lost forever, just because of some ali'i's greedy demands."

"You know a lot about this stuff. Maybe you should be the docent?" Estelle said.

"Ha! Even as tour guide, I still used little cards and have websites bookmarked on my phone. It's the only way I survive most tours." The time had come to push her agenda. "Do you think you could do me a favor and check with Margaret to see if she has a few minutes to talk with me? It really is important."

"Um, yeah, I could check. There aren't any tour groups coming through in the next few minutes. Wait here," Estelle said, before turning to leave.

"Wouldn't it be easier to call Margaret on the phone?" Maile asked.

"Margaret's sort of different. She doesn't like to be interrupted by phone calls."

Keepers of the Kingdom

While she waited, Maile looked at the exhibits again, today with a new eye as to why someone would want to steal them from a church. A couple pairs of tourists came through, and she eavesdropped on their conversations. Mostly it was about where the feathers came from, why not just use a flag like everyone else, followed by where they would eat dinner that evening.

When Estelle returned, Margaret came with her. Maile got her next surprise of the day when she saw the museum curator she thought she'd known since a kid.

Chapter Five

Maile blinked away confusion. She wasn't sure if she was looking at her fellow congregation churchgoer. "Margaret?"

"Yes. You're Maile Spencer, right?"

"Yes. I wasn't sure…I guess it's been a while since I've seen you…since we've met…since…how've you been?"

"Great, thanks. Made a few lifestyle changes, as you've undoubtedly noticed. Still working as a nurse?"

"I have some time off from that." Maile was looking for a diplomatic way of finding out about Margaret's lifestyle change. Dressed in a button-down shirt and khaki slacks, and with a manly haircut, she looked much more masculine than feminine. And with the way her shirt wasn't filled out the way Maile would expect, there had been a lot of changes. "How long has it been since we met at church? A couple of years?"

"Probably about that. Surprised?"

"A little. I hadn't heard about your changes," Maile said. There were so many things she wanted to ask.

"I doubt anyone at that little church knows anything. Can you imagine the gossip that would go around if they saw me like this?"

"I think they'd be glad to see you there, no matter what. Anyway, I have a few questions about the kahili here at the museum. I heard from Estelle you got a new acquisition."

"A pair of late nineteenth century kahili. Very good condition."

"Any way that I could see them?"

With the way Margaret was scanning Maile's face, she felt as though she was being scrutinized for something more than mere appearances.

"To what end?" Margaret asked.

"Sometime since last night, the two kahili at the Kawaiaha'o Church were stolen, or at least removed, and no one knows where they've gone. I'd just like to see your new ones, if maybe they're the same."

Margaret led Maile off to a small conservation lab in another part of the building. "Yellow feathered drum with red upholstery below? Six foot pole?"

Maile's hopes were up. "Sounds right."

"Keep looking. I don't have them." They got to where two small handheld kahili were clamped in vices in the lab. "As you can see, my new acquisitions are black and all feathers. Not even close to being the same as those at Kawaiaha'o."

It was another letdown for the day. "Rats. Okay, well, do you have any idea who might be in the market for large decorative kahili?"

After aiming a light, Margaret put on a set of jeweler's loupes and perched on a stool to give a close examination of her new acquisition. "Nobody would make much noise looking for something like that. Things like these are moved through online black market auctions. Know much about those?"

"A little." In fact, Maile had helped recover a historical Hawaiian artifact a few months before, and some of her research had involved black market auction sites. "Just to look, not to buy. I never realized how much stuff there is out there."

"For the right price," Margaret said. "Almost seems like there's more on the market than in museums. If only I had the financial backing to buy it all."

"You think my best option would be to check all the auctions?"

"Three of the best are Polynesian Profiteers, Dream Acquisitions, and Secret Substitutions. If you come across a site named Bounty Mounties, they're actually law enforcement experts pretending to be buyers looking for the jerks that are selling the stuff. The smaller sites that you'll find are mostly fences looking to turn a profit, quick and easy. You can tell those sites because they'll sell almost anything, including guns and ammunition. Don't even look at those. You don't want those cookies on your computer."

"Would a black market site have the Kawaiaha'o kahili listed already? It hasn't even been a day since they disappeared."

"They get the stuff listed as soon as they get it. They don't want to store it, just turn it over to a buyer. They probably just keep the stuff in the garage. A lot of the time, they already have a buyer and a deal has been made, and use the online site simply as a way of letting the buyer know it's available."

That gave Maile a few things to think about. "Thanks. I guess I'll concentrate on that. I don't know what else to do at this point."

"Are the cops involved?"

"They've taken a report, but I doubt they'll spend much time investigating. There's something of a time constraint, with a big wedding tomorrow morning. I was hoping to have them back to the church by then."

"Yes, I read about the Fortuna wedding in the newspaper. Sounds like the biggest wedding of the year. I've never been able to figure out why anyone would want a giant affair like that. Find a priest, say I do, and get it over with, if you ask me."

"I'm one of the bridesmaids," Maile said.

"Should be fun."

"I hope so. Any ideas on the kahili?" Maile asked.

"My suggestion is to figure out who might be most interested in buying a pair of kahili and look for them. Find the buyer, and you'll find the fence, and that's when you'll find the thief. That's how the black market works."

"Good idea." Maile couldn't help but notice Margaret's hairstyle, still wondering what brought on the changes. "Will I see you at church sometime?"

Margaret flipped up the loupes and looked at Maile. "I don't go by Margaret in my personal life. I'm Mark now. How do you suppose those people would deal with that?"

"Only one way to find out." Maile shrugged. "Come as Mark. You can sit with me and my mom."

Margaret went back to work on the black feathered kahili in front of her. "Thanks."

With fresh ideas to guide the rest of her search, Maile decided on putting two more hours of work into trying to find the missing kahili. Once again, she hoped that's all it was, that they were simply missing and not stolen. Maybe they'd been removed for cleaning and no one was informed, or put in storage for some reason. Neither Reverend Akamu nor anyone else at Kawaiaha'o Church seemed to know anything, all of them shrugging their shoulders over the puzzle. Even though Brock Turner had taken a report, the police weren't terribly concerned. The best she could do was to search the internet for black market sites that might be selling them. If by the time dinner rolled around she hadn't found them, she'd give up. She had a bridal shower to attend that evening, and planned on having more than just one glass of wine. In fact, she had a secret stash of money set aside to take a taxi home from the party.

Just as she was turning the key in the ignition to start her car, she remembered the girls.

"Yeah, nice job, Maile. Leave the kids behind to fend for themselves. Granddaughter of an ex-President and a runaway from...wherever she came from. Where're their mothers, anyway?" While walking back to the kids' garden center, she got out her phone. "Sammy's mother isn't coming in until tomorrow morning, which means if I want to go to Lani's party tonight, I need to find a sitter for Sammy." She hit the first number in her phone list. "Mom, can you do me a big favor tonight?"

"Need me to fix your bridesmaid dress? Too big for it already? Let it out?"

"What? No. If anything, it could be taken in a little around the waist. I need a sitter for this evening."

"You make a baby I never heard about?"

"Mom, I really need this favor." Maile explained about Sammy being a runaway and how her mother wouldn't be coming in until the next morning. "I really want to go to Lani's place this evening. Actually, I *need* to go to that party, just for the wine and talk story with old friends. You mind much watching Sammy?"

"Nobody invited this ol' lady to the party, so I guess I can."

"Come on, Mom. I feel guilty enough dumping the kid on someone else. She's a sweet little girl and won't be any trouble, I promise."

"Haole girl?"

"She's from somewhere in the Midwest. I doubt there're many Hawaiians there."

"What's she eat?" her mother asked.

Maile got to where she'd left the kids in the hands of museum employees and no one was around. Trying to keep panic from setting in, she stepped up her pace and started to circle around the building. "I don't know. Whatever Midwestern kids eat. Hot dogs, I guess."

"You bring your mother some groceries, a bag for the kid and a bag for me, and she can stay with me. But not all night. Not runnin' a boarding house. What time you come pick her up?"

"The party is from seven. Maybe ten o'clock? That's not too late?"

"Should be awake. Bring some popcorn for us. We'll watch TV."

"Not supposed to have salt...never mind. I'll bring her by at six-thirty."

Maile still didn't see any kids, or museum workers that might've been leading a garden activity, but a volunteer was stacking chairs on a trolley. She looked unhappy about something.

"Pardon me, but I'm looking for a pair of girls that were part of a garden activity earlier. You know where they are?"

"That ended half an hour ago. All the parents already came to get their little miracles."

Maile checked the time and noticed she wasn't that late. "But there should be two more kids that haven't been picked up yet. Two ten-year-old girls."

"Maybe they were the ones that left with some lady?" the volunteer said.

"What lady? Where'd they go?"

"Off over there toward the visitor parking lot."

Maile looked but saw no one. Only the nearly empty lot and the planetarium. "How long ago was that?"

"I dunno. Half hour?"

"Who was the lady?"

"I dunno."

Maile began running toward the parking lot. "You don't know much, do you?"

"Hey! At least I didn't lose my kids!"

Maile was focused more on the lot than anything else as she ran past the planetarium. Running so fast, she ignored the trio of workers in a flowerbed, until she heard young voices call out to her.

"Oh, there you are!" Maile said when she spotted the girls. One was holding a garden hose while the other used a trowel to dig holes in the dirt. A woman was there with them, also planting bedding flowers. Their shoes and socks were on the ground a few feet away.

"I'm the lead gardener and the one who puts together the outdoor activities for kids at the museum. You must be Maile?" the woman said, looking out from under her wide-brimmed straw hat.

"Unfortunately," Maile said, now looking at the mess the girls had made of themselves. "What's going on, anyway?"

"The group activity ended a little early, and since you weren't around, I recruited your friends to help me with this. I told one of the volunteers to wait for you."

"Is it time to go?" Thérèse asked, holding her trowel. She had dirt up and down the front of her shirt and shorts. The biggest mess was the mud that clung to her legs.

"Who are you? Mud Monster from Planet X?"

Thérèse giggled. "Maybe!"

Maile shook her head at the mess. She also knew she would've been in the same condition at that age. "Well, Keepers of the Kingdom, it's time to go."

"Me, too?" Samantha asked. Water was pouring from the end of her hose indiscriminately, creating a giant mud puddle at her feet. She wasn't any cleaner than Thérèse.

Maile tried not to laugh. "Yes, I guess I have to take you with me. But there's no way you're getting in my car looking like that. It might be an old wreck, but I'm not turning the inside into a garden."

Thérèse and Samantha made their way out of the muddy flowerbed while Maile held the hose and apologized to the gardener for the mess.

"They've been a tremendous help," the gardener said, chuckling as she watched the girls wipe mud from their clothes.

When they started to put shoes on over muddy feet, Maile remembered the hose in her hand.

"You can't put shoes on over muddy feet."

"It's okay," Thérèse said. "These are play shoes."

"My feet have been dirty before," Samantha added.

"Yeah, you know what?" Maile aimed the hose at the girls, which brought squeals. Spraying them down to get the mud off them was helping, even if it was soaking them through. Soon, the squeals turned to laughter, the gardener joining them.

"Gonna get the seats wet," Samantha said as they walked to Maile's car.

"I have a couple of towels to use. Anyway, wet's better than being muddy. Did you guys have fun?"

"Yeah!" they said in unison.

"That garden lady showed us how to plant flowers."

"She let me use the hose to water them," Samantha said.

"They got plenty of water, that's for sure."

"Did you find the kahili things?" Thérèse asked once they were in the car.

"Not yet." Maile watched them with her rearview mirror as they got seatbelts buckled and continued to dry themselves. "Time to go somewhere so you can take showers and we'll wash your clothes. By then, it'll be time for Sammy and me to eat dinner, and Thérèse, your mother should be on Oahu by then."

Thérèse seemed to wince a little. "Gotta go with my mom? More fun with you."

"I'm sure she wants you back." Maile got the car started on the first turn of the key. "Certainly able to take better care of you than I can."

Chapter Six

Instead of taking them to her tiny apartment for baths, Maile took the girls to her mother's cottage in Manoa Valley. The first place Maile went, as always, was to the large screened aviary at one end of the backyard where her pet cockatiel lived.

"Since you guys are a mess, you can help me clean King's house," she told them.

"Who's King? Another boyfriend?"

"King is the best boyfriend ever." After the three of them went in, Maile held her arm out to one side. "King, come."

The bird fluttered his wings and left his perch in a back corner. When he awkwardly landed on her arm, the girls backed away.

"He's big!" Samantha announced.

"Why's he fly wrong?" Thérèse asked.

"He gets his wings clipped occasioanlly so he can't fly away. This way, he can go outside and look for stuff to eat while I clean his house."

"He'd fly away?"

"He did once. He was gone for a week. I was heartbroken, too."

"Does it hurt?"

"His wings getting clipped? About as much as getting a haircut." Maile got the tools to clean the chicken wire aviary. "Since you guys are Keepers of the Kingdom, you can clean King's castle."

"How do we do that?" Thérèse was holding the shovel while Samantha had the putty knife.

"One of you uses the putty knife the scrape his perches while the other uses the snow shovel to scrape the floor."

"Gotta scrape poo?"

"Yep. That's one of the jobs of a Kingdom Keeper, to scrape bird poo."

The girls negotiated that since Samantha knew how to shovel snow, she'd clean the floor while Thérèse scraped perches. Maile took King out to where he fluttered to the lawn and landed with a thud. Seeing him flutter almost to flight, she knew it was just about time for his trip to the pet store. While watching him root through bushes for living snacks, she listened to the girls talk about their work.

"Never thought I'd have to do chores when I got here," one complained.

"All you have to do is scrape. I have to shovel this stuff."

"Never knew one bird can make so much poo."

"Just think how much poo turkeys make."

"Must be a lot."

"You guys eat turkey on Thanksgiving?"

"We're vegetarians."

"Oh, yeah, I forgot. What do you eat on Thanksgiving?"

"Stuff. Tofu, noodles, rice, vegetables, potatoes, yams."

"No turkey?"

"We're vegetarians. What do you guys eat?"

"Not tofu."

"Thanksgiving is next week. You'll be home by then. Too bad you can't come to our house."

"I'll be locked in my room for like forever. If it snows, we'll make a snow family."

"My mom goes surfing while my auntie cooks."

"Your mom doesn't cook?"

"She's not so good in the kitchen."

"My mom likes to cook. That's why her bu...never mind."

Hearing enough schoolyard gossip, she took the crate of avocados from Detective Ota to the kitchen and left a note on them about who they were from.

Maile had the girls collect everything in a bucket and toss it in a compost pile. Since they were already wet and dirty, and she was still protecting her fancy nails, Maile had them spray the aviary with the hose and fill King's food bowls. She found him in the vines along one fence and told him to stay in the yard.

"He obeys you?" Samantha asked.

"He knows who feeds and loves him, so yeah, he obeys. Better than men do."

Her mother wasn't home, but there was a grocery list on the counter. While the girls played rock paper scissors to see who would shower first, Maile tossed their wet clothes in the laundry washer and set it to heavy duty. She dug through boxes of old clothes until she found the smallest shirts and shorts for them to wear. She still wanted to snoop online for websites dedicated to the black market sales of Hawaiian artifacts, but was short on time. Somehow, she needed to shop for groceries, drop Thérèse off with her mother in Waikiki, finish the laundry, and shower and dress before going to Lani's party. She'd have to look at a computer in the

Manoa House now if she wanted to spend any more time on her search.

She peeked into the bathroom and set the stack of clothes on the counter. "I'm going next door. Take your showers and put these on. Please don't make a mess."

"We won't," they promised.

"Once you're dressed, clean up your mess and come over to the big house next door. Thérèse, you've been there before. Come in through the patio door, okay?"

"Okay."

"Please don't make a mess in here." Maile started to shut the door but opened it again. "And don't waste water."

That's when one of them pushed the door closed, locking Maile out. She hurried over to the Manoa House next door.

"Seriously, if there's a mess in there later, Kingdom Keepers' heads will roll."

With her mind half on the kids and half on her search, she logged onto the internet using the fastest computer in the library. She wasted no time in researching background information about those two kahili missing from the church, and went straight to plugging in the names of black market sites Margaret had suggested.

"Okay, let's see what's available at Polynesian Profiteers."

She needed to set up an account to be able to search, which required a name and email address, including a credit card number.

"No way am I giving them my real name." It took barely five minutes to set up a fake email account using an alias. Back at the black market site, she needed to provide personal demographic data, along with a credit card number. She also knew that the IP address of the computer would be scrutinized by the site. "Hello, Richard Nixon of Honolulu. That'll be sure to catch someone's attention, which means I need to work fast."

She used every search term she could think of: kahili, feathered standards, ancient feathers, Hawaiian artifacts, church artifacts, and several more before giving up. Just as she navigated away from them and started deleting cookies, the girls came in through the patio door.

They stood at attention. "Are we okay?"

"Yes, very clean. Your hair is even combed."

"No mess in the bathroom, either."

"Where'd you hide the mess?" Maile asked.

The girls looked at each other for the answer. "Have to tell you?"

"I'll find it eventually."

"In the washer."

"The clothes were done, so we moved those to the dryer and put the towels and other stuff in the washer."

"What other stuff?" Maile asked.

The girls looked at each other. "Dirty stuff."

"Thank you." Maile gave them permission to look through drawers at old artwork and documents, after prying promises not to tear anything. She still wasn't satisfied there wasn't a mess at the cottage, and now worried that the laundry room was being flooded by soapsuds pouring from the washer. When indigestion boiled up that tasted like Chinese food, her patience was tested. "Okay, I need to go check on the laundry. Can the two of you stay out of trouble for that long?"

The girls froze. "Maybe we should go do that?"

"You're sure you know how to use those machines?" Maile asked.

"Just like at home, right?"

"I help my mom with the laundry all the time."

"So do I."

Maile took a deep breath, wondering if she was inviting even more trouble. "Okay, fine. When the dryer is done, change into your own clothes and put the towels in for thirty minutes on medium heat."

"We know how to do it," one of them said on their way out the door.

Maile turned her attention back on the computer. "Yeah, just like you knew how to water a flowerbed."

She was required to set up an account at Dream Acquisitions, using the same email and personal demographics as earlier. That took as long as it took the girls to move the clothes from the washer to the dryer and return.

"There was a lady there," Samantha said.

"My mother?" Maile asked. It was still a little early for her to get home from work.

"I dunno."

"What did she look like?"

"Not too tall. Long hair wound around a bunch of times on top of her head," Samantha said.

"Hawaiian lady," Thérèse added.

"That's my mom. Were you nice to her?"

"Of course!"

"She gave us cookies."

Maile turned around to look at them. They had one cookie each, the same as what Maile and her brother Kenny had got as kids. "I don't know if that's a hundred percent vegetarian, Thérèse."

"It's okay. I know the brand. Mom gets the same ones."

"You need to wash your hands before you touch anything."

"Just took showers!" one of them said.

"That was before cookies. I don't want the oil from the cookies getting all over old documents."

"Can we look at our phones?" Thérèse asked.

"You can have your phones back when your mothers get here."

"So strict," one whined.

"Prison warden."

Maile turned back to her computer to hide her smile from them. "Welcome to the Spencer House for refugees."

This next website seemed to have a much bigger inventory of "lost" items for sale, and she interpreted that as meaning stolen. While she searched the website, the girls poked through drawers and cabinets in the library.

"Sammy, by the way, my mom and you are spending the evening together. I have somewhere to go for a couple of hours later. You can eat popcorn and watch TV together. I hope you like old movies."

"I don't need a babysitter."

"No, but you do need a guard. I don't want you running away again. You're in enough trouble with your mother. Better not mess with mine, or the trouble really starts."

"Not gonna be any trouble."

"What about me?" Thérèse asked. "Do I get to watch old movies, too?"

"I'm expecting a call from your mother any time now." Maile picked up her phone. "In fact, I'll call her right now."

It took several rings before the call was answered.

"I was just going to call you in a few minutes," Dr. Kato, Thérèse's mother, said. "I have a problem here on Maui I'm contending with."

"You're still on Maui? What time will you be in Honolulu?"

"Not till tomorrow morning, I'm afraid. Are you able to put Tay on a plane? I can have someone pick her up here when she gets in."

Maile did her best to keep her curses in the Hawaiian language. "I'm busy this evening and all day tomorrow. I was hoping to drop her off with you pretty soon."

"This was completely unexpected or I never would've sent her early. I've learned my lesson. I'm really sorry. I don't know what to tell you, Maile."

"What's wrong?" Thérèse asked. She'd found her way to Maile's elbow.

"Your mom's not able to come here till tomorrow. I guess there's some big emergency on Maui that she needs to deal with as mayor."

"I hafta go to the hotel by myself?"

"No, but you'll need to fly home alone, just like how you got here this morning. Is that okay?"

"Why don't I just stay the night with Sammy and you?"

"Okay, this isn't a hotel, and I don't have the space..." Maile thought of the bridal party that evening, and taking Thérèse to the airport was just one more time-wasting errand. "You know what? That's a good idea." Maile told Dr. Kato about Thérèse's idea, framing it as a sleepover. "They could share my old bedroom, and both my mother and me would be here with them."

"Them?" Dr. Kato asked.

"Yeah, there's another girl from Iowa spending the day with us."

"Maile," Samantha said, tugging at Maile's sleeve.

Maile ignored her and explained about how Samantha was an 'unexpected visitor' and how the girls got along so well.

"Maile," Samantha said, tapping Maile's shoulder with a fingertip.

"Just a minute," Maile whispered to the girl, before going back to the call. "Mom's cottage isn't a luxury hotel, but it's safe and dry, and they have a bed to sleep in."

"That's what she has at home. Three hots and a cot," Melanie said.

"Maile..." Samantha insisted, bouncing her finger on Maile's shoulder.

"What?"

"I'm not from Iowa. I'm from Ohio."

Maile went back to her call with Dr. Kato. "I'm supposed to tell you Sammy is from Ohio, not Iowa. Apparently, that's important." They hammered out the details, of tooth brushing, bedtime hour, and a reminder about vegetarian food. "Anything I need to know?"

"Just that sleepovers rarely go as planned," Melanie said, chuckling.

"Guess what?" Maile announced after the call. "Big sleepover at the Spencer house tonight!"

Once the excitement of that subsided, and a new list of rules was handed out, Maile was able to dedicate some time to her computer search while the girls occupied themselves with the library. It was a matter of clicking from one image of something up for illegal auction to the next image, searching for the missing red and yellow kahili. She was lost in a world of her own, wondering how much money she would need to buy back all the Hawaiian history that was for sale. It wasn't until the girls fell silent, and one of them said something about something they'd found being 'so cool' that she turned around to see what they were doing.

They were both seated on the floor cross-legged. Thérèse was just handing a koa wood paddle to Samantha, something decorated with sharks' teeth along the edges and a feathered lanyard at the opposite end. The bottom drawer of the cabinet next to them was open, with dried ti leaves scattered across the floor.

Maile almost jumped from her chair. "What're you doing with that?"

"Nothing."

"What is it?" Thérèse asked. "It's funny looking."

"It's an old paddle and there's nothing funny about it." Maile tried wresting the ancient artifact from Sammy's hands, but she wouldn't let go. In fact, she was waving it in figure-eights in front of her. "It's not a toy. It shouldn't even be out of its drawer."

"I'm not playing with it! It's doing that by itself!"

Maile watched as the paddle continued to wave through the air. "Try setting it down."

"It won't…I can't…" Samantha's worried look grew. "It's getting hot, Maile!"

"I know it is." Maile grabbed the girl's hands and clutched them in her own. That calmed the waving and she was able to settle the paddle into the girl's lap. She felt the heat emanate from the koa wood through Samantha's hands. "Just relax, okay?"

"I'm scared, Maile."

"So am I, a little. Thérèse, can you do me a favor and go out in the garden and get some ti leaves for us? You know what those are, right?"

"We got 'em at our house." Even Thérèse looked suspicious of what was going on, scooting backward until her back was against the cabinet. "How many?"

"As many as you can carry. There's some scissors in the desk drawer for you to use. And get a piece of the maile vine from the flowerbeds." Something else stabbed at her mind. "And don't run with the scissors!"

Once Thérèse was gone from the room, Maile needed to proceed with her problem of not being able to unlock Samantha's grip from the paddle.

"Look, I know this is really scary for you, but there's a secret about this paddle I need to tell you. It's such a big secret, that I sent Thérèse away so she wouldn't learn it."

"I can't let go," Samantha said. Tears were beginning to form and a lip quivered. "It's getting hotter."

"Just relax, okay? I think it knows you're afraid and is reacting to that. Just try to calm down a little."

"It knows about me?" the girl asked.

"I think it knows stuff about you that even you don't know. We'll figure that out later. Right now, you need to try and relax your grip on it."

"What's the secret?" Samantha asked.

"First, you need to promise never to tell anyone, not Thérèse or even your mom. Not that they would believe you."

"I promise, if it'll stop doing this."

"Many, many years ago…"

"Like a hundred?"

"Like thousands. There was a man named Maui." Fighting time, Maile gave a brief recap of the story of the demigod Maui, how he'd used that specific paddle to propel a canoe across the ocean with his brothers, and used a fishhook to snag the ocean floor. "Hauling in his fishing line, he pulled up the Hawaiian Islands. That's the hook that's inset into the face of the paddle."

"That's Moana's story," the girl said.

"Disney's version, anyway. But it's really the story of Maui."

"Maui was like a god or something, right?"

"A demigod. His mother was a god, and that fishhook was made from one of her bones, and the feathers on there were from birds that led them across the ocean, just so they could find Hawaii. So, in a way, this thing is still alive with the spirits of the gods inside of it."

"That's why it's waving around?"

Maile nodded. She now had Samantha seated in front of her, her arms around the girl, still holding the paddle. "And why it gets so warm. The funny thing is, it usually only reacts to Hawaiian people touching it."

"Can you make it let go of me now, please?" the girl begged.

Thérèse was just coming back in with two handfuls of ti leaves.

"You need to keep your promise, or other bad things might still happen," Maile whispered in Samantha's ear. It might've been overly dramatic and overdone, but Maile was grasping for straws at that point.

"I promise."

Maile got a large leaf from Thérèse and wrapped Samantha's hands with it.

"Okay, try to let go now."

"I can't!"

"Wiggle your fingers one at a time and see what happens."

By letting go one finger at a time, the girl was able to release her grip on the koa handle and scooted away in a hurry. Both girls watched as Maile held the paddle in her lap. Keeping a firm grip on it, she felt its struggle to move about on its own.

"Okay, take out those old leaves and make a bed of new leaves at the bottom of the drawer." She watched as the girls complied. Once the drawer was prepared, Maile wrapped the paddle in the red and yellow silk fabric that had been tossed aside, while the girls watched intently. She used the old strand of maile vine to tie the silk together and set it on the bed of leaves. After layering the remaining leaves on top, she had one more task to do.

"Okay, I have to say a prayer in Hawaiian and the two of you have to be quiet while I do that. Understand?"

"Yes."

"Uh huh."

Maile chanted quietly, hoping the moment wasn't turning into a sideshow. When she was done, she set the fresh strand of maile vine on top of the bed of silk and ti leaves.

She waved for the girls to come close. Once they were close enough that she could hear them breathing, she looked back and forth between their eyes.

"I think both of you are smart enough to never talk about this. Am I right?"

"Yes," they said in unison.

"I'm sorry we played with the paddle," Thérèse said.

"Me, too," added Samantha.

"Thank you for the apology, but you have more apologies to make."

"To God?"

Maile shook her head. "I already talked to the Hawaiian gods. You guys need to talk to the paddle."

She listened as both girls made contrite apologies to the paddle, or at least put on a good show of it. Then she closed the drawer. Throughout the process, she muttered something under her breath.

"Was that Hawaiian language?" Samantha asked at the end.

"Yep."

"What'd you say?" Thérèse asked.

"A prayer."

"For what?"

"I asked the gods to keep inquisitive hands away from ever bothering the paddle again."

"Sorry," Thérèse said quietly.

"Yeah, that was weird," Samantha said. "Why'd it wave around like that?"

"Because it was angry someone was touching it."

"But it stopped when you held it," Samantha said.

"Maybe because it's okay if I do, but not for others? I don't know why."

"Authorized use only," Thérèse muttered. "You put the maile vine in there because of your name?"

"Because I'm supposed to be protecting it, yes." Seeing the girls begin to relax, she wrapped up her lecture. "I hope that was a lesson learned, that when you go to someone else's house and they tell you to leave things alone, they have their reasons."

"You want us to clean up this stuff?" Thérèse asked about the old ti leaves on the floor.

"Please. There's a broom and dustpan in the kitchen."

Maile figured they learned the lesson since they swept the entire floor of the room, one using the broom, the other working the dustpan. What impressed her most of all was how well two strangers had bonded so easily.

"You guys go over to my mom's house. If she's in the kitchen, don't get in her way. She's not very agile anymore. I need to go to the supermarket. I'll be back in a few minutes."

Maile didn't know what else to do with the dead leaves she found in the wastebasket, so she tossed them in the compost pile with King's manure and lawn clippings, wondering if they should've been burned during prayers instead.

"There must be a protocol for something like that."

Chapter Seven

Half an hour later, Maile was home with four bags of groceries, enough to feed half a dozen kids. Dinner was already on the stove, and the girls were seated at the kitchen table looking hungry, but well-behaved. While they chatted about school life in their respective hometowns, Maile took a quick shower and dressed in something she had set aside for that evening's bridal party. At the store, she'd splurged on two extra bottles of wine, wiping out the remainder of her weekly food budget. Those she'd left in the car for Lani's party.

Just when her mother was scooping large helpings of rice, vegetables, and beans onto plates for the girls, Maile took her aside.

"Okay, so, there was some trouble at the Manoa House this afternoon."

"I heard all about it," Kealoha said. "About something doing some tricks? What was it?"

Maile wondered if the time had finally come to let her mother in on the secret of Maui's paddle being hidden in a cabinet drawer at the Manoa House next door.

"Doesn't matter what it was." She took a deep breath and slowly blew it out. To prevent ten-year-old eavesdropping ears from listening, she spoke to her mother in Hawaiian. "Remember when I was a kid and you made me promise to never bring it up that you're kahuna?"

"Why for you to bring that up now? You know I don't like talking about it."

"This is important. I need those girls to not remember what they found, or where they found it. Can you do that?"

"That thing so important as all that?" Kealoha asked.

"You have no idea."

"I need to know what it is."

Maile whispered the answer in her mother's ear.

"For real?"

Maile nodded.

"Okay, I do it. Some conditions, though."

"I figured there would be."

"Be home early tonight. No driving after too much drink. And no playing around with boys."

"Mom, I'm old enough…what makes you think there's going to be guys there?"

"I went to those parties. I also know that Lani girl isn't so wholesome."

"What? What do you mean by that? You've known Lani all her life."

"That's why I know she's not so wholesome."

"Either am I. Married and divorced already by age twenty-seven. What's that say about me?"

"Doesn't matter what it says. All that matters is what you say about yourself. You sleep with too many boys at a party, you get yourself a reputation."

"Didn't I get this same lecture about a dozen times when I was a teenager?" Maile asked, switching back to English.

"Maybe it's time to hear it again."

"Okay, I'll be home early. Both girls are supposed to be in bed by nine. I should be home not long after then." She grinned at her mother. "Unless I can find some boys to play with."

"You're going out now?" Thérèse asked.

"Leaving us behind?" Samantha added.

"Sure am. Just remember that neither of you were supposed to spend the night here, and that you're guests at my mother's house." She leaned down to look both of them in the eyes. "If either one of you causes trouble for my mother, you're both in big trouble with the Hawaiian gods. Got it?"

"They won't be any trouble at all," her mother said, as if she had something hidden up her sleeve.

Maile was glad to leave the girls behind in the care of her mother. She'd left them with popcorn and kids videos to watch. Whether or not they got in bed on time was her mother's problem. Finally pushing the last thoughts of two ten-year-olds ruling the roost at her mother's little cottage from her mind, she parked near Lani's apartment in a Waikiki high-rise. She was looking forward to a giant release of emotions while talking story with her oldest and best friends, to laugh and cry, and feel the warmth of a glass of wine in her cheeks. To everyone's surprise, not only was Lani's mother at the party, but the groom's mother, also.

Even though Lani's heritage was mostly Filipino, she got her family name of Fortuna from her Portuguese ancestors. Just like so many people in the islands, she also identified as Hawaiian because of the few drops of Polynesian blood that flowed through her veins. All day long, Maile had wondered why the two kahili were so important to her, and she could only assume she wanted them in her wedding to celebrate that part of her heritage. It had turned out to be the biggest wedding of the year at the Kawaiaha'o Church, and Maile was proud to be in it.

Lani's groom, though, was as white as Lanikai beach sand. They'd discovered each other two years before when he'd crashed a Christmas beach party at Ala Moana Park. While he'd found a pretty island girl, she'd found a sugar daddy. Lani was coming from money of her own, new money that was found in real estate sales of land that had been abandoned after the cane fields closed. Not only their wedding was a big event, but the merger of the Fortuna's and the Stickney's bank accounts in the world of Honolulu business was even bigger news.

Even with the elegant gowns, the abundance of flowers, and the giant reception, Maile still wasn't convinced the marriage wasn't much more than a business merger. But that wasn't her problem, at least not right then. Maybe after they come back from their honeymoon…

Ten minutes into the party, and Mrs. Stickney was lost among the various languages being spoken by the bridesmaids and a few of the other guests. It didn't help that most of the food there was Filipino, often an acquired taste for people from the mainland the way Mrs. Stickney was. She had a twist to her polite smile as though there was a bee in her bonnet, and learning why was going to be as much fun for Maile as any party games played that evening.

"Okay, Mrs. Fortuna and I have an idea about the party," said Mrs. Stickney. As many times as she'd been begged to relax and call everyone by their first names, she continued to sit upright and address everyone formally. "We think it would be fun to send each of you on a treasure hunt."

Lisa, the maid of honor, was just getting the cork out of a bottle. "Huh?"

"Treasure hunt?" Lani asked, looking at her mother. "I don't remember talking about that. I thought we were just going to sit around and drink and play stupid party games?"

"Yeah, I want to tell lies about the good old days," Lisa said.

"Mrs. Stickney has been very persuasive," Mrs. Fortuna said. Maile didn't know the woman very well, but could tell from the smile on her face that it was forced. "It's like an old-fashioned scavenger hunt."

"What kind of scavenger hunt? You want us to find tennis rackets and purple slippers?" one of the bridesmaids asked.

Mrs. Stickney produced a sheet of paper. "We have a list…"

"Personally, I'd rather find a guy," Maile said, taking a sip of her wine.

"A guy as in Brock Turner?" Lani asked. "I wouldn't mind finding him on a scavenger hunt!"

"These days, any guy that knows how to brush his teeth without dribbling on his shirt would be good enough!"

"You know what would be fun?" Lani asked the group. "If we all drew straws for a type of man to find."

"Yeah! Someone in uniform. We all have to get kissed by a guy in a uniform, and get a selfie of it for proof."

"Different kinds of uniforms. One of us needs to find a police officer, another a firefighter, someone else needs to get kissed by a soldier."

"Sounds like fun!" Lisa said. She got a napkin and started scribbling notes. "Who else wears a uniform?"

"Doctors, male nurses…"

"The concierge at a hotel…"

"Security guards, mall cops…"

"No, not mall cops. The malls will be closed pretty soon anyway."

"Okay, we have our list," Lisa said.

"How do we decide who gets the firefighter?"

"Lani should get the firefighter."

"Sounds good to me!" Lani said. "Or maybe Sergeant Brock Turner, if Maile doesn't mind?"

"Why should I mind?" Maile said, felling a pang of jealousy.

"Who is this Brock Turner?" Mrs. Stickney asked through a tight smile.

"Oh, just a police officer that's been sniffing around Maile for the last few months. And from what I've heard, she's been sniffing back!" Lani said.

"Well, we have our list of things to find…" Mrs. Stickney said, going back to her sheet of paper.

"Let them have their fun," Mrs. Fortuna told her.

"My future daughter-in-law wants to find men to…do things with!"

"Just a simple kiss," Lisa said. "Not a third date."

"Mrs. Stickney, I'm marrying your son tomorrow and spending the rest of my life with him. Just once more in my life I'd like to be kissed by a man before it's too late."

Mrs. Stickney sat back with her arms folded, her list of scavenger hunt items on her lap. Mrs. Fortuna didn't look much happier about the change in plans.

"Okay, final set of rules," Lisa said. "We all have to get kissed by as many men in uniform as we can. Doesn't matter who they are or what kind of uniform they're wearing. Just a kiss and a selfie before moving on to the next guy."

"Maile has one guaranteed kiss, anyway," Lani said.

"Brock Turner, here she comes!" Lisa announced, as Maile got ready to leave.

"Too easy!" someone said. "Maybe she should find someone else?"

"Yeah. She'll just get a dozen kisses from him and win the contest!"

"Can we talk about someone else, please?" Maile begged, feeling her face flush red.

"How much time do we have, anyway?"

"Two hours. Whoever has the most kiss selfies, wins."

Whatever the others did to find men, Maile's mind was set on Brock as she walked to her car. She still wasn't convinced the game hadn't been rigged. Once she was in her car, she gave Brock a call, her hands shaking a little as she dialed.

"Yeah, hey, howzit, Brock?"

"Maile, aren't you at the bridal shower, or whatever it's called?"

"We're having a scavenger hunt of sorts."

"You're not still looking for those kahili, are you?" he asked.

"Kinda gave up on those. I have something else to talk...see you about. Where are you?"

"I picked up a half shift of work this evening. I'll be off duty in a couple of hours. Can it wait until then?"

"I guess. Where should I meet you?" she asked.

"Come by my apartment. You know where it's at?"

"That place in Kaimuki, right?" The only reason she knew was because Detective Ota had pointed it out to her on one of the times he was driving Maile somewhere.

"Yeah. If you get there early, my brother will let you in."

"You have a brother?"

"And a sister. You didn't know?"

"I remember something about your sister going to the mainland for college and never came back. I never knew you had a brother."

"He's quite a bit older than me. He's been living with me for just a few weeks now. He likes the neighborhood. Anyway, I need to go write a traffic ticket. See you in a couple."

With two hours to kill and some nerves to settle, Maile wondered who else she could pry a kiss from that wouldn't turn into trouble. She considered finding a concierge on duty in Waikiki, but thought better of it. As a tour guide that frequented hotel lobbies, she couldn't risk her reputation.

"Well, someone said something about doctors and nurses being fair game." She started her car. "I know a lot of them."

Ten minutes later, she parked in the Emergency Room lot at Honolulu Med, the place she used to work.

She had her mind made up of who she was going to approach, that of Dr. Howard, an older gentleman ER physician and widower that had always treated her kindly. She was hoping he'd understand the game and play along without making too much of a fuss over it.

Before going in, she called her mother to check on the kids.

"We're eating popcorn and watching Disney," Kealoha said.

"Which Disney?" Maile was hoping it wasn't Samantha's favorite, Moana. She still slipped up every now and then and called Maile Moana.

"Some princess thing. It's cute."

"Everything's under control?"

"We're fine. Go have fun with your friends."

Going into her old workplace, Maile had her eyes set on Daniel, a male nurse, someone she suspected would play along but not take her kiss seriously.

The department wasn't busy and both men were on duty that evening. She found Daniel restocking a cabinet. She also discovered someone else had found him before her. Lani was there, along with Lisa, the bride and maid of honor. They'd decided to go on the scavenger hunt together, since Lani had had too much to drink to drive her own car.

"Come on, brah!" Lisa said in a nagging voice. "We explained the game to you. All we need is one quick kiss and to get a selfie of it."

"Please?" Lani begged.

When Maile got to them, she could tell he was making himself too busy at doing nothing to avoid their request. "I have too much work to do to play games."

"What, you got a girlfriend around here someplace that might get jealous?" Lani asked, her hands on her hips.

"I just don't like those kinds of games."

"What about me, Daniel?" Maile asked. "I'm in the game, too. Would you kiss me?"

"Oh, hi, Maile. It's a real game?"

"Unfortunately, yes," she said.

"And three women are standing in line to let you kiss them," Lisa said. "You gonna help us or what?"

The whole scene was just a little too weird for Maile's tastes, and she just wanted to get it over with, without watching as Lani and Lisa pried a favor out of him. Since she'd seen them at Lani's apartment, they'd both put on more makeup and lipstick.

"Since you know me, maybe I can go first," Maile offered.

"Just on the cheek right?"

"Gotta be on the lips, brah," Lani said. She was turning out to be a lot more aggressive than Maile would've guessed. Maybe what her mother said about her was right. "It's the rules."

"The lips? Really?" he asked.

"Big ol' wet one, right on the kisser," Lisa said.

Daniel turned around and began his cabinet stocking activity again. "Forget it. I don't know you guys well enough."

Lisa and Lani departed in a huff, off to look for someone else.

"What about me?" Maile asked. "You know me well enough?"

"I…I don't…maybe…"

Maile pulled the privacy curtain so they could be hidden. "Daniel, I'm not going to take advantage of you. It's just for Lani's stupid game."

"She's the one getting married?"

"Yep."

"I feel sorry for her husband." Eyes as big as saucers, he looked at Maile. He cornered himself when he backed into the wall. "Okay, sure, I guess it's okay. You have to take a picture?"

Maile got her phone. "Sorry. Part of the deal."

"Will you delete it later?"

"I promise."

Holding her camera to one side with one hand, she put her other hand on his shoulder and leaned in. She was surprised when he didn't try to wiggle free. He kept his eyes open. Maybe she was lost in the moment, or maybe it was curiosity, but the tip of her tongue slipped forward and touched his lip. All that accomplished was bring an end to the kiss.

"Get your picture?" he asked, looking at the screen on her phone. He almost had a look of disgust on his face.

"Got it, thanks."

"Not going to show that around too much, right? Not going on social media?"

"I promise." She touched his cheek with her hand. "Your secret is safe with me."

Having the first one under her belt loosened her nerves a little. Starting to have fun with the game, she found Dr. Howard in a cubicle jotting a few notes. She explained the game, and he agreed to something on her cheek. Before that happened, she sat with him for a while, discussing when she was coming back to work at the hospital.

"I think the dust needs to settle in the rest of my life before I can make any realistic decisions. I just got through with my divorce, and on the heels of that, my ex-husband has landed in hot water with the District Attorney about something with his business, I'm not sure what. Then I still have some weird thing going with the US District Attorney and a prince from the Middle East, and I'm waiting on hearing from the State Licensing Board about getting my nursing license back."

"That's a full plate. You're earning a living as a tour guide?" he asked.

"It's becoming more lucrative."

"Well, we're all waiting for you to come back as soon as you can."

"Honestly, I'm just trying to get through this stupid scavenger hunt and the wedding tomorrow without making too much of a fool of myself."

"It all sounds like good fun." Sirens blared outside in the street, and the flashing lights of an ambulance reached to where they were seated. "Looks like we have a customer. I suppose I should fulfill my part of the agreement."

She knew he meant the kiss. "Never mind. Having the chat with you was everything I needed this evening."

A patient that had obviously been in a car wreck was whisked by as Dr. Howard walked Maile to the exit. An ER team intercepted the patient being brought in by paramedics, and guided the parade to a trauma bay. To Maile, Dr. Howard hadn't changed a bit in the several months since she'd worked there, letting the crew handle their tasks and manage the patient until it was time for him to step in. Leaving him and the crew behind, Maile went off in search of her next adventure.

"Forget it," she muttered, getting her car started again. "Ones from Daniel and Brock will have to be good enough. Let the others do whatever. I'm not even sure I want one from Brock now."

Sitting in her car, she called her mother again.

"Getting ready for bed. No need to call so much, Maile girl," her mother said. "Raised two kids of my own. I know what to do."

"Been a while since your raised us. Might be out of practice."

"Managed you, didn't I? If I could do that, I can manage these little angels for one night."

Maile drove to the small, older apartment building in Kaimuki, a residential area of mostly houses near central Honolulu. It was a concrete building with a stucco façade, painted a fading pink, only half a block off the main street that went through.

She found *Turner* on the mailboxes, and it indicated the top floor of the building. Looking up, all she could see was one apartment at the top, with a small rooftop patio next to it. In any other situation, she'd consider it a loft or penthouse, but not in that older building. As she climbed the stairs to the top floor, she wondered what Brock's older brother might be like.

Chapter Eight

After she knocked on the door, Maile listened to clattering noises that came from inside.

"Just a minute!" There was more clatter, something repetitiously banging or rapping on something else. "Maile?"

"Yes. Brian?"

The door opened slightly. She saw the security chain across the gap. It was dark inside the apartment. "Maile Spencer?"

"Yes. I'm sorry, did I wake you? Brock told you I was visiting this evening, right?"

He opened the door the rest of the way, still leaving his face in the dark. He smiled. "I've been expecting you. Please come in."

Only one small light was on in the apartment, and quiet music was playing. A modern computer on a desk in a corner glowed with life, and a few potted plants decorated corners of the room. The furnishings were basic, no-nonsense, in an easy to clean apartment. Two closed doors led to other rooms, one she suspected being a bedroom, the other the bathroom. It's what she would expect for a bachelor police officer to live in, but not nearly big enough for two brothers.

"Can I get you something to drink?" Brian asked, moving slowly to the small kitchen. It was a real kitchen, unlike hers, with cabinets, a full-sized fridge and stove, and a window that looked out to the street. "I heard you like ginger ale? I hope so, because I just got back in from a trip to the corner grocery."

"That's fine, thanks." Something peculiar was going on, that he wasn't turning on lights for her, and moving through his paces at such a slow speed. Was Brock hiding in a corner somewhere, ready to jump out in a surprise? She hadn't seen his pickup truck on the street outside and surprises like that didn't fit Brock's personality. She watched as Brian carefully dropped ice cubes into a glass and pour a little of her drink. He hadn't bothered to turn on the kitchen light when he went in. "Is Brock home yet?"

"He just called and said he'll be another hour or so. I guess there's some sort of crash on the other side of town." He left the kitchen brushing past her as he went. "There should be space on the couch for you to sit. Make yourself comfortable."

Still with few lights on in the apartment, Maile sat at one end of the couch, holding her ginger ale. "I hope it's not a serious accident. I was just at the hospital a few minutes ago and the first victim was just arriving."

"Brock said you used to be a nurse. You're working as a tour guide now?"

"Yeah, used to be." Maile sipped. "These days I'm trying to figure out how to be a successful tour guide."

Brian eased down into the swivel chair at the computer, found a key on the keyboard and gave it a tap. After, he turned to face her. "That would be fun for a while, but I bet going to the same old places all the time gets tiresome."

"It does." With the computer right behind him, she still couldn't see much of him. It wasn't that she distrusted him; it was a matter of sitting in the dark with a stranger. "Brian, would it be okay if we turned on another light?"

"Of course!" he said cheerfully. "Put on as many as you like. I forget I have them turned off sometimes. Not that it matters much."

Maile turned on the lamps on the end tables on either side of the couch she was on. That's when she finally got a good look at his face. He had a couple of dense scars on his cheeks, and his eyes weren't focused on anything in particular.

"Oh, you're blind. I didn't realize that. Brock didn't say anything."

"He usually doesn't make a big deal of it. It's easier for me that way." He tapped his hand on the computer. "You're probably wondering about this, how I can use it. I have a voice to text program to write."

"You use it a lot?"

"I have a couple of blogs that earn me money, and write books."

"What kind of books?" she asked. She'd discovered reading was a good way of filling time between tours.

"Poorly edit ones with lots of typos."

"Because of the text to voice program?"

Brian shook his head. "Because I speak one way and books are written in a different way."

"That's interesting." Maile sat sipping her ginger ale, wondering how to proceed. She'd taken care of patients that were blind, but had never socialized with a blind person. "Okay, I'm not sure…"

Brian interrupted. "Brock said you're on some sort of scavenger hunt in a bridal shower?"

"Oh, yes. It'll sound very silly to men. The women at the party were sent to get kissed by men in uniform. Any man, any uniform. The one with the most kisses captured on selfies wins."

"What do you win?"

"An embarrassing reputation."

"Maybe so." He chuckled. "How many do you have so far?"

"One." She thought of Daniel's insincere smooch. "I guess it counts."

"Brock is supposed to be one of them?" Brian asked.

"That's the idea. I'm running out of time for it."

"Maybe I can help?"

"I, well…"

"You could get a two-fer with me. I could put on my old firefighter uniform, and my old Army uniform. They're hanging in a closet around here somewhere."

"Thanks, but I'm not really trying to win the game. I should be getting back to Lani's apartment soon, anyway."

"It sounds like a big wedding tomorrow. You're Brock's date for it?"

"Not exactly a date. We're opposite each other in the bride and groom's sides." Her curiosity finally overwhelmed her. "How did you become blind? Something related to being a firefighter?"

"Combat in Iraq. I was a firefighter for just a couple of years when the war came along. I joined up, served a couple of tours, and just before I was due to come home, I was injured in an explosion. Eventually, I was sent all the way back to Tripler Army Medical Center, but they couldn't help me much. I've been to the VA hospital half a dozen times, but because of budget cuts, I'm on a waiting list to be seen by an ophtha…eye doctor."

"How long have you been on the waiting list?"

"Fourteen years."

"What? How can they make you wait so long?"

"Nobody will tell me for sure, but I think there's some sort of notation in my chart that I'm a hopeless case. The scar tissue on my eyes is too dense, or something like that. I can sense light and movement, but that's about all. I'm okay getting around at home, but I need a cane when I go out."

"How long have you lived here with Brock?" she asked.

"Just a few weeks. I'm still finding legs of tables with my little toes."

"Sorry."

"Doesn't matter." Brian smiled. "I don't use them for anything else."

"It must be hard to…"

He stood. "You want those selfies now?"

"With you in your uniforms? I guess it would be okay."

"Look, I know you and Brock have the hots for each other. I'm also not some sort of pervert trying to kiss a pretty girl. All I'm trying to do is pad your total a little. You want the pictures or not?"

"Sorry. I didn't mean to hurt your feelings."

He went into the bedroom and left the door ajar. "You sure are sorry a lot."

Maile gave her answer some thought. "You're kind of blunt."

"I don't like beating around the bush." When he came out of the bedroom, he had on a dark firefighter's uniform shirt. "Mainly because I can't see the bush very well."

Maile stood. "I never know if I'm supposed to laugh when you say things like that."

"If it's funny, you laugh. Have your camera ready?"

"We're doing this now?" she asked, straightening her dress for some reason.

"Rather wait for my brother to get home so he can watch?"

She ran her tongue over her teeth, sweeping them clean. "I guess we better do this."

"Now there's something that inspires a lot of confidence."

Just like with Daniel, Maile held her phone to one side before leaning in. Unlike with Daniel, she was met halfway. The kiss lasted longer than she expected, and was much warmer than what Daniel had offered. When they finally parted, she got something of a shiver.

"Get the picture?" he asked.

Maile remembered she had the phone in her hand. Looking at the screen, she realized she never snapped the image. "Yeah, got it. Thanks."

He left the room to change clothes again. "I heard something about the kahili being missing from the church? What's that all about?"

"That's what I'd like to know," she said. She touched a fingertip to her lips, wondering if what just happened had been real. "I mean, who steals something like that?"

Brian came out of the bedroom again, this time wearing a green uniform shirt from the Army. This one had more buttons and insignia on it than did his firefighter shirt. "I think you need to look for someone who has the most to gain from something like that."

"I've looked at several black market websites. It's not for sale that I can see."

"They might not have stolen it for the money. Unless it's worth thousands, it wouldn't be worth the risk. That's how it was when the museums in Iraq were raided during the war, that thieves took only the things that could be moved offshore quickly and for a large profit. All the minor stuff was left behind for souvenir hunters."

"I'm not sure if kahili are minor or major," she said. "Or how much they'd be worth."

"Ready?"

"For?"

"You want another kiss, right?"

"Oh, yeah." For some reason, Maile slipped her phone into her pocket. When they leaned in close to each other, she took him in her arms and held him close. This time, she didn't let him go until she was done.

"Get the picture?" he asked.

"Uh huh."

"How? Sure felt like you were all hands with that one."

"I got what I needed."

Brian went back to the bedroom to change clothes again. "The value of those kahili might not be monetary. Somebody might want them for something other than for turning a profit. That might be what you need to focus on."

Not knowing how she got there, Maile discovered she was sitting on the couch again when Brian returned to the room. He sat on the couch, not quite at the far end from her. "What do you mean, something else besides monetary value?"

"Who could gain personally by having two kahili?"

"Well, they'd be rather odd things to have as decorations in a house, and anybody that had ever seen them at the church would recognize them in someone's living room. They'd be too difficult to ship. Customs inspectors would question their origin if they saw them."

"Why did you mention customs inspectors?" he asked.

"They'd have to go through customs if they were shipped internationally, right?"

"Yes, but what made you think they'd leave the islands?"

"Like I said before, they'd be too easily recognized here. I doubt many people on the mainland would be interested in them. If they were leaving the islands, they'd have to go to a collector of things like kahili."

"Hate to keep pushing the agenda, but who would collect something like kahili? What's so special about them that someone would steal a pair of them from a church?" he asked.

Maile was still trying to shake the kisses from her mind, and couldn't focus on his questions. "Well, they're objects of royalty. Maybe somebody likes to collect things of royalty?"

"That might be the thread you need to pull on and follow." He turned a little to aim in her direction. "Who's getting married tomorrow?"

"One of my oldest friends, Lani. I'm discovering a few things about her this evening I never knew before."

"Like what?"

"Like her mind is more dedicated to Ronald than her body. Or soul."

"You think that because of the kissing game?" he asked.

"She's going at it pretty enthusiastically. Maybe I'm an old frump, but...I don't know."

"Will it be a big wedding?"

"Giant. It's at the old Kawaiaha'o Church, and the place is covered with flowers and garlands. Big reception at an expensive hotel with tons of people there. And then a week at Disneyland for a honeymoon."

"Not any of my business, but who's got the money to pay for all that?" he asked.

"Both families, but Lani's is footing the bill for most of it. I think half the reason she's marrying Ronald is for his earning potential." Maile shook her head and silently scolded herself. "I can't believe I just said that."

"Nothing unusual about people marrying for money, or power. It's possible to have a little too much of both, though. What're the in-laws like? Will everyone get along?"

"Mrs. Stickney, the groom's mother, is a real prize."

"Why?"

"Oh, the bridesmaids just wanted to sit around and talk this evening. She was the one who came up with the idea of the scavenger hunt."

"So your friend Lani allowed her future mother-in-law to change the plans of her last party with her friends as a single woman?"

"Putting it like that, it doesn't sound so good. She also wasn't invited to the party, nor was Mrs. Fortuna. Somehow, they showed up."

"Kinda manipulative, if you ask me," Brian said.

"Very. The odd thing is that Lani was in tears this morning over the missing kahili, and this evening she's looking for guys to kiss her. Not once has she mentioned Ronald's name all day. I don't get that at all."

"You're sure there's actually going to be a wedding?" he asked, laughing. It was the same laugh as his brother, Brock. She looked at the time, wondering where he was.

"Flowers have been arranged, the decorations are up, gowns and tuxedoes are ready to be worn, and fake fingernails have been glued into place. What else is there other than 'I do' and some over-priced jewelry?"

"I've never been married, but the whole idea of marriage is premised on the condition of love, isn't it?"

"You sound like a lawyer, writing up a contract," she muttered.

There was the clatter of a key in the front door, and Brock came in. Maile practically leapt from her spot on the couch.

"Find the place okay?" Brock asked, after greeting both of them. Before much could be said, Brian left them alone and closed himself in the bedroom. "Did I interrupt something?"

"Huh?" Maile straightened her dress for some reason. "No, we were just talking about the missing kahili and tomorrow's wedding."

He dropped his keys and wallet in a bowl on a small side table. After that, he unloaded his pistol and stowed it in a locked drawer. "Get any answers?"

"A few things to think about. How was your shift?"

"Car accident on the H-1 that just cleared. Sent a few patients to your old stomping grounds."

"I saw one a while ago."

He aimed for her to sit on the couch. "What were you doing there?"

"Oh, just playing this silly party game." Instead of sitting, she edged toward the door to leave.

"Oh, yeah, that game. What'd you need from me?"

Maile pursed her lips and tasted Brian's kiss again. "I think I already got it."

"Good. Was my brother a good host?"

"Um, yeah, great."

"He give you anything?"

She wondered if he sensed something lingering in the air. "Anything?"

"To drink."

"Yes, ginger ale."

"Did something happen? You look flustered," he said.

"No, everything's fine. I just need to get back to Lani's place."

"Haven't been drinking? You're okay to drive?"

"Just the ginger ale." She noticed the closed bedroom door. "Maybe I should say goodbye to Brian before I go?"

"He's in bed."

"Already? It's not even eleven o'clock."

"Early to bed, early to rise is Brian's motto. He stayed up late to entertain you."

"I thought I was a fuddy-duddy," she whispered.

"There's something you need to know before you hear about it on the news."

"Don't tell me. Kawaiaha'o Church burned down?"

He looked startled. "What makes you say that?"

"I don't know. Just feeling a little on edge about tomorrow. What shouldn't I see in the news?" she asked.

"You know at the Iolani Palace, in the King's Bedroom, there was the quilt on Kalakaua's bed?"

"What do you mean, was?"

"It's been stolen."

"Huh?"

"Sometime this evening, after the docents went around to check on all the rooms, and before the first check by the night watchman. Gone. Detective Ota has had a crime scene team there all evening looking for fingerprints and stray evidence."

"That's terrible. Who would steal something like that?"

"Same kind of person that would steal kahili from a church. You know Ota is going to ask you eventually, so I may as well ask now…"

"Do I know where the quilt is?" she said. "Not a clue. I'm still trying to figure out what happened with the kahili. But just like you and Ota always tell me, it's not my problem to solve."

"When was the last time you were at the palace?"

"Three days ago for a tour. You can check their logbook. They keep track of tour visits. Does that let me off the hook?"

"That's up to Detective Ota."

"It would be pretty hard to smuggle a quilt out of the building when so many people were around." She opened the door to let herself out. "See you at the wedding?"

"You need a ride there? I can come pick you up," he offered.

Ordinarily, she would've jumped at the chance, mainly because she wasn't sure if her car would start in the morning. As things were right then, Lani's wedding the next day was the furthest thing from her mind. "I should be okay."

Getting out to the sidewalk, Maile went to a convenience store for a snack. She found her favorite comfort food, chocolate mini-doughnuts and milk, and sat in her car eating one after another.

"This is totally not on my diet. Three weeks before running a marathon, and I'm eating this stuff." She tossed another doughnut in her mouth. "But what was that all about with Brian? Did that actually happen?"

Looking at the pictures on her phone, she decided to delete Daniel's picture, deciding his privacy was more important than the game. After that, she called her mother.

"In bed but whispering to each other," Kealoha said, even before Maile could ask. "Coming home soon?"

"Not too long," Maile said, chewing on a doughnut.

"What are you eating? Serving dinner so late?"

"Having a doughnut."

"Serving doughnuts for dinner?"

Maile put the last of her sweets in the glove compartment. "Just having a snack."

She was the last to return to Lani's apartment. There was a little too much estrogen blowing through the room while Lani and Lisa shared the selfies saved on their phones.

When it came to their turns, Lei-lei and Jenn had nothing to share, saying they'd spent two hours eating French fries in a fast food joint.

"All I got to say is that there better not be any wardrobe malfunctions at my wedding tomorrow," Lani said. "How many did you get, Maile?"

"I struck out, also."

"What about the one from Daniel?" Lani asked.

Maile needed an excuse. "After you guys, he wasn't interested in me."

"Oh, that guy," Lisa said. "That was like kissing a dead fish. What about Brock?"

"Yeah, what about him?" Maile said.

Lani kept searching Maile's phone for selfies. "Where's the big kiss?"

"Oh, he had to work an extra shift this evening."

Lani tisked and handed back the phone. "You're hopeless."

It wasn't hard to feign a yawn. "I should go. I'll need to get a run in the morning to sweat off some extra calories if I have any chance of fitting into my gown tomorrow morning."

"Sure you're not headed back to the Turner apartment to sweat them off there?" Lisa asked.

Brian's kisses floated through her mind. "If only I were so lucky."

With the kids spending the night at her mother's cottage, Maile needed to return there. But her gown for the wedding was at her apartment, and she likely didn't have enough time in the morning to meet the kids' mothers, go home to shower and dress, and then go to the church a couple hours early to be with Lani on her big day. The morning hours before the ceremony would certainly take on a different complexity than what the party had that evening, with nerves all around. The faces on the two future mothers-in-law, Mrs. Fortuna and Mrs. Stickney looked calm enough, but didn't look as though they'd spent much time bonding that evening.

Maile decided she was too tired to get any more involved with Lani's future family dynamics and called it a day. Her one and only stop was at her tiny apartment near the university to get her gown, shoes, and anything else she might need in the morning.

Most of the lights in the building were already off, making the place look even gloomier than what it really was. Going down the hall, she heard late night activities come from the room of someone she suspected earned a living the old-fashioned way. As she unlocked the series of locks and deadbolts in her door, her neighbor's door opened. Rosamie, the young wife, popped her head out.

"That you, Maile?"

"One and only."

"Where you been all evening?"

"Out with friends. Sorry, but I don't have time to talk right now. Kinda tired."

Rosamie came out into the hall and followed Maile into her room. She was wearing a sheer nightie, with another sheer cover over it, not enough coverage for outside the bedroom. The only modesty was what her husband's boxer shorts provided. "You look nice."

"I look like I need some sleep."

"Get your brows done?"

"They're that noticeable?" Maile asked. She wiggled her fingers. "And these."

"Of, yeah, big wedding in the morning. Hey, someone came by looking for you earlier."

"Mrs. Taniguchi looking for rent money? Because it's not the first of the month yet."

"Not her. A guy."

"Oh?" Maile wondered who it might've been. She'd seen Brock, and Detective Ota would've been at the Iolani Palace investigating the theft of the quilt. Her brother couldn't be bothered with visiting except when tuition time came around. Her tour van driver Lopaka was undoubtedly at home with his family. Otherwise, they were the only men in her life who knew where she lived. "I hope he was tall, dark, and handsome."

"I don't know. Not my type."

Maile hung her gown still in its plastic dry cleaner cover on the doorknob. Rosamie, for as interesting as she normally was for gossip, was proving to be a pest right then. Standing so close to her, Maile got an eyeful of her friend's figure through the sheer fabric, and everything that went with it. "Okay, what type was he?"

"The type that kept banging on your door. I finally had to ask what he wanted."

Maile went off in search of the shoes that went with the gown. "Can you give me a hint as to who he was?"

"Didn't say his name. He had some big package to deliver, though."

Maile tossed her shoes down at the door and went in search for a makeup and perfume pouch she'd already arranged for the next day. "I haven't ordered anything that needed to be delivered. What company was it from?"

Rosamie touched her finger to her chin in thought. "Maybe not from a company. I got the idea it was a personal thing."

"Probably got the wrong address." Maile collected her gown and everything else, ready to leave for her mother's house. "Running out of time, Rosamie. If you know who he was or what he had to deliver, now's the time to tell me."

Her friend shrugged. "I dunno. Just some guy wanting to give you something. He said he'll be back."

Maile maneuvered Rosamie out the door and began the long process of setting all the locks. "I'm sure he will be."

"Hey, tomorrow's the big day!"

Maile looked at her watch. "Actually, tomorrow has turned into today, and the bags under my eyes are growing by the minute."

"The wedding's at the big Hawaiian church downtown, right?"

"Everyone's welcome to attend church there." Maile had to fake a step in one direction to step around her neighbor in the other, just to get past her. "Just as a suggestion, you might want to wear more than that nightie when you leave the apartment, Rosamie."

That got a little distance between them and Maile was able to go down the hall toward escape.

"What's wrong with it?"

"Nothing, in the bedroom. Sort of husband's eyes only, if you know what I mean."

Chapter Nine

When she got to her mother's cottage, the same place that she'd grown up in, her mother was still up and in the small living room. Her sewing machine had been taken out and set up on the desk, with a strong lamp aimed at it. Scraps of fabric were here and there on the desk and floor, and a small muu'muu was hanging on a hanger suspended from a curtain rod. Kealoha was sitting in her favorite chair, working on a project, sewing something by hand with needle and thread. It was the exact same scene Maile had seen a hundred times as a kid. Her mother had grown beyond middle age, but the charm was as strong as ever.

"A little late to be working on that, isn't it, Mom?"

"Needs to be done by morning. How was the party?"

"Oh, you waited up for me. I didn't get drunk, or do anything else, if that's what you're worried about."

"Worried more about you not getting enough male companionship."

"It's all about Lani this weekend. Who're the dresses for?"

"Your little friends."

Maile looked at the dress hanging from the curtain rod. It was a small muu'muu, with a subtle Hawaiian floral print. She recognized the fabric as leftover from something that had been made for her many years before. "Thérèse and Sammy? How are they? Did they get to bed on time?"

"Very good girls. I should've raised one as well-behaved as them."

"I didn't know I was so troublesome. Why are you making them dresses?"

Kealoha bit the thread and set the needle aside. She held the dress up for a look. "So they can go to the wedding."

"Lani's wedding? Why are they going to that?"

"Because they've been invited."

Maile sat knock kneed in a chair across from her mother. "I don't understand. Both of them are going back to their mothers first thing in the morning. I've been assured of that. The wedding isn't until noon. Why are they coming to the wedding and how did they get an invite? Lani doesn't know them, or their mothers."

"Maile girl, you need to learn to relax. First, Mrs. Fortuna called me to say hello and asked if I wanted to come to their place this evening to meet the new in-law. Then when she heard about the girls staying with us for a while, she invited them to the wedding. They no can go to wedding in shorts and T-shirts, so I'm sewing something for them."

"Okay, they're not staying with us for a while, they're out of here tomorrow. One's going home to Maui, the other to Idaho."

"Ohio."

"Wherever. As long as they go."

"Had a nice chat with Sammy's mother."

"How'd you know her phone number? Oh, you gave back their phones. Did she call Sammy, or Sammy call her?"

"All that matters is they worked out their problem. Very nice lady. Turns out that Sammy is part Hawaiian."

That got Maile's attention. "How much?"

"Someone in her father's family came to the islands many years ago, and took home a wife and baby. Small branch on a big tree. I think she made the story nicer than what it is."

"So, that explains…"

"Explains what?"

"Nothing." Maile stood to leave the living room for an overdue shower. "And I'm not tense."

"I didn't say tense, Maile girl. I said you need to relax."

Maile stopped. "Mom…never mind."

By the time she was out from her shower, her mother had gone to bed. The lights in the cottage were off, and the couch had been turned into a bed for her to use, with sheets and a blanket. Stretched out on the lumpy mattress, she had time to think about Lani's wedding, and her future life with Ronald. He seemed like a nice enough guy, career driven, always on the lookout for new business opportunities. That was the good news for Lani, and Maile was happy her friend would live a life of ease.

But to Maile, Ronald wasn't the warmest guy in the world. They'd dated for only a year before he popped the question, and that took place over burgers in a fast food joint. The ring was nice, if a little utilitarian with no inscription inside, a little bit of a letdown since he was able to afford something a little more grandiose. He hadn't participated in any of the wedding plans as far as Maile knew, and seemed mostly along for the ride. If it had been her, she'd have put the brakes on the wedding a long time before.

"But what do I know? I'm already divorced," she whispered, before dozing off.

***

The scent of coffee and the clink of spoons in bowls woke her in the morning. Maile had a backache from sleeping on the thin mattress, and one hip was sore from resting on some sort of bar all night. It was too late to go on the run her body craved. Flinging back the sheet, she sat on the edge of the bed and rubbed the cobwebs from her face. Listening to the girls in the kitchen chat about the wedding while eating what was probably oatmeal or mush, Maile put her wavy hair in a long braid.

Looking at her phone, there were no calls or messages. The biggest problem right then was that it was already after eight o'clock. She still needed to shower, dress, put on her face, do her hair, and wrangle her mother and the girls into her car for the drive to the church, all in the next two hours.

And with a pounding headache.

"Hi, Maile!" the girls said in unison, and a little too cheerfully, when she joined them at the table with a mug of coffee. There was something green on their plates that looked like guacamole from the evening before. With a crate full of avocados, she figured she'd be eating a lot of them in the coming days.

"I heard you were good girls last night. Thank you for minding my mother."

"She said we can call her Granny Kealoha," Samantha said.

"You may call her Auntie. Unless you want trouble with me."

"She also said you're not so tough," Thérèse said.

"Oh, really?" Maile got a bowl of mush for herself, and more coffee.

"Yeah, she said you're a softy," Samantha added.

"Maybe she's right, but if I were you, I wouldn't push my luck. Not today."

"Yeah, big wedding today!" Samantha said.

"We get to go!" Thérèse said.

"Our moms, too!"

"Where'd you hear that?" Maile asked.

Thérèse seemed to wince a little. "Kinda talked to them last night."

"Again this morning," Samantha said.

"Yes, I heard you got your phones back. Did your mothers get to Oahu okay?"

Both girls nodded.

"Granny…Auntie…your mom said our moms can come to the wedding," Samantha said. "Is that okay with you?"

"Okay with me, but I'm not the bride. We can't start inviting more people to a wedding, especially ones the bride and groom don't know. And Sammy, you're still in the doghouse. I'm not so sure you should be allowed to go to a wedding."

"We'll be quiet," Thérèse said.

"And behave," Samantha added.

"Well, I'll tell you one thing that's not going to happen, that's your phones ringing. If I hear either one of your phones even chime during the ceremony, do you know what's going to happen?"

"Nuthin'?" Thérèse asked.

"Glare at us?" Sammy said.

"At least." Maile took their bowls to the sink and ran water in them. "Might take both of you to the Buddhist convent for the nuns to deal with you."

"My mom said my grandmother almost joined the convent when she was young," Thérèse said.

"Good for her. Tell Sammy about it," Maile said, shuffling from the kitchen, taking her mug of coffee with her. She passed her mother in the hallway as she went to the bathroom. She was already dressed for the trip to the church later that morning. "You look pretty, Mom."

"Are you showering now? I'll get the girls dressed."

"I'll get them. It's my job, and I want to have a little pep talk with them."

"Don't give them too many of your rules. Just keiki, after all. Need to let them have fun. Good to have happy keiki at weddings."

After showering, Maile put on the makeup the way Lani's personal 'bridal advisor' suggested, and dressed. By then, the girls were in the bedroom, trying to decide who was going to wear which dress their new hanai auntie had sewn for them.

"Okay, Thérèse, the blue dress would look better on you, and the green dress would be better on Sammy with your blond hair and green eyes."

The girls traded dresses and began slipping into them.

"You have green eyes?" Thérèse asked.

"Like, duh."

"Be nice, please," Maile said, trying not to scold. She tried getting the twist in her hair right, but it kept flopping apart. Deciding to leave that for later, she looked through her bag for the jewelry she was supposed to wear to the wedding. "Hey, either of you been in my bag today?"

"Not me."

"Unh uh."

"I'm missing some jewelry. You haven't seen it?"

"Nope."

"Not me."

Kealoha came in. "Ready to go? It's about that time."

"I'm missing my jewelry."

"I have something you can wear," her mother said.

"It's a necklace that Lani gave the bridesmaids. Just loaner stuff that's paste, but I need to be wearing it for the ceremony. We're all supposed to have the same things on." Maile finished digging through her bag. "Maybe I left it at my place. We'll have to stop there on the way."

Everybody got their shoes on, and taking as little as possible except for Samantha's knapsack and their phones, they went to Maile's car. Once everybody was buckled in, Maile turned the key in the ignition.

Nothing happened.

"Come on. Not today."

Maile got out and popped the hood up. Finding the usual troublesome engine part, she gave it a slap before getting in and trying to start it. Again, it wouldn't start.

"Well…"

"Careful. Keiki in the car with us," her mother warned.

"Maybe it's time for them to learn some new words."

"Already know those words," Thérèse said.

"I'll teach you new ways of using them."

"Know that stuff, too," Samantha said.

After a few more futile attempts at starting her car, Maile gave up and got her phone.

"Calling taxi driver?" Kealoha asked.

"Something like that." She waited until the call was answered. "Howzit, Brock. This is Maile. I have a problem."

"Car won't start?"

"How'd you know?"

"Seems to be your luck lately. Need a ride to the church?"

"At least. First, I need to go to my apartment to get something that I hope is there and not lost. There's four of us. Can you fit all of us in your pickup?"

"Should be okay in my quad cab." They waited in the shade of a tree near the front of the Manoa House. It took him all of ten minutes to get there. Her mother sat in the back seat with the girls while Maile was in the front with Brock. "I talked with Brian this morning."

"Oh." A sense of dread sailed through Maile, wondering if their secret had been divulged over breakfast. The excitement of the kisses in the dark room had passed, and her thoughts of romance had returned to Brock and the evening they were sure to spend together. "How's he?"

"Fine. He wants to know if it's okay if he calls you sometime?"

"I…huh?"

"You know, for a date."

"Brian wants to go on a date with me?"

"Yes. You, him, table, chairs, coffee, talking."

Maile was confused. It was the wrong Turner interested in taking her out. "I guess it's okay."

"Do it, Maile!" Samantha said.

"Yeah, go for it," Thérèse added.

"I agree," Maile's mother said in Hawaiian. She smiled broadly. "One good Turner is as good as the other, as they say."

"Maybe it's something for me and, well, Brian to figure out, and not a panel of critics."

Brock parked in front of Maile's apartment building. Everyone in the pickup looked more at the hooker strolling the curb than at the building.

"I like her outfit," Samantha said.

"We don't got girls like that on Maui," Thérèse said.

"You guys stay here. I just need to get one thing," Maile said. Her mother began to open the door to the sidewalk. "Where you going, Mom? You don't need to chase her away."

"Why not?"

"She's been living in my building the last few weeks."

"You know her? I wonder what her name is?" Samantha said.

"Happenstance."

"That's her name or her position in life?" Brock asked. "Not position, but…"

"I know what you mean. Her working girl name is Happenstance."

"Must be new in town. Never met her before."

"I want to see your place," Maile's mother said.

"You know where I live."

"Never brought me inside."

By then, Thérèse and Samantha had met the streetwalker and were busy making friends by asking about her 'costume'. Brock also seemed interested, and Maile wasn't sure if it was from a legal police point of view, or as a man. She decided to ignore him and get the girls away from the professional waving at cars going by.

"Kids, let's go!"

Samantha had her nose curled up when the kids came back. "Needs a bath."

Maile led the group up the stairs, her mother at the front, the kids in the middle, and Brock bringing up the rear. Thumbtacked to her door was a note, something about a delivery being made too early in the morning and to see Mrs. Taniguchi as soon as possible. As she went through the procedure of unlocking the door, Rosamie came out to meet them.

"All dressed up for the wedding!" the neighbor lady said, after learning their names. She waved for Maile to step away. "Maile, come."

"In a big hurry right now, Rosamie. I'd love to hear about the kids and your husband, but can it wait till tomorrow?"

"Not about them." She took Maile partway down the hall. "Hey, you got some weird friends."

Maile nodded her head at the group waiting for her. "Them?"

"No, they're cute. I'm talking about the ones that were here this morning."

Maile looked at her note from the landlady again. "Did someone make the delivery?"

"Old lady Taniguchi let them in. Weird stuff they dropped off, too."

"Like what?"

"You'll see."

When Rosamie's husband called for her, she darted back into her apartment, leaving Maile with a new set of qualms. She had no idea what had been delivered or was waiting inside her room, and she was about to open the door to see it, along with her mother, Brock, and two little friends. Since she was running late and still needed her jewelry, she worked the last lock and swung open the door. The surprise was bigger than she ever could've expected.

Keepers of the Kingdom

Chapter Ten

Maile's headache caught up with her again. Her frustration with everything came out verbally. "What the…"

"Never heard that word before," Samantha said quietly. Thérèse cupped her hand whispered something in Samantha's ear. "Oh."

Maile's mother kept the girls at the doorway while Brock and Maile went in. "Did you know this stuff was here?" he asked.

"I had no idea," she said, standing back to look at what had been arranged over and on her bed. "It wasn't here last night."

"What time was that?"

"Right after I left your place. A little after midnight."

Brock found a little notepad and pencil that had been hidden in a tuxedo pocket. She wondered where he had his gun hidden. "You're sure it wasn't here then?"

"Brah, I think I'd notice two kahili over my bed and a royal quilt covering it."

"Those are the kahili that belong to Kawaiaha'o Church, right?"

"Or very good imitations. And I'm pretty sure that's Kalakaua's quilt, from Iolani Palace."

Kealoha pushed past them to feel the fabric and look at the stitching close up. "This is it. The real thing. Why's it here?"

"I have no idea, Mom."

"Don't touch anything." Brock started taking pictures of the arrangement with his phone, right after calling for a squad car and an evidence team.

"Can I at least get my jewelry for the wedding?"

"Where is it?"

"In a kitchen drawer."

"The kitchen?" he asked.

"I put it beneath the knives and utensils. Seemed as good as any place, not that there are many places to hide something here. Ever since Mrs. Taniguchi took my fan again, I have nowhere to hide valuables."

Brock looked confused. "You hide valuables in a fan?"

"Long story. Can I get the jewelry or not?"

"Yeah, sure. Just don't touch anything else."

"You live here, Maile?" Samantha was now wincing as much as Thérèse was. "I thought you lived in that big house next door to your mom."

"I wish."

"Why do you live here? It's so small."

"Believe it or not, tour guides don't make much money. Mom, can you take the kids outside to the sidewalk. Maybe you can give Happenstance a lecture about personal hygiene?" Once they were gone, Maile set her eyes on the feathered Kalihi that were crossed over the head of her bed, and the colorful red and yellow quilt that was spread across the mattress.

She got a text on her phone from Lisa, asking where she was, that she missed breakfast and the photographer was taking pictures of everyone. She ignored it, since she didn't know how to reply.

"Was the bed down from its storage place inside the wall?" Brock asked, still taking pictures from various angles.

"I always put it up before I leave home. It just makes it more spacious in here with it put away."

"Anything else different in here?"

"As in?" she asked.

"Anything missing, or added?"

"From what I can see from here, nothing is missing. Not that I have much." She got another text, this one from Lani. "We need to get to the church, or at least I need to."

Maile's phone beeped with a call. It was Lisa's number, the maid of honor. "Are you in this wedding or not?"

"I'm running a little late. Sorry."

"Please tell me you're late because you found Brock last night and are having trouble getting out of bed?"

Maile put the call back on private, stepped into the hall, and pressed the phone to her ear. "There's Brock and a bed, but not in the way you're thinking."

"Where are you?"

"My apartment."

"Well, there you go! But finish up with him so both of you can get to the church. Lani's getting nervous."

"We've run into something of a problem." Maile explained about the church's missing kahili being found in her apartment, along with the stolen quilt from the palace.

"I saw that on the news, about the break-in at the palace. How do you get into so much trouble?"

Maile wanted to laugh at the question. "I don't know. I'm hoping that as soon as police officers get here, they can take over from Brock and we'll get to the church on time. I mean for Lani's wedding."

"Let's get Lani married and worry about you and Brock later," Lisa said, laughing.

There were a pair of sirens outside that silenced when the police cars must've stopped at the curb. A couple of minutes later, two uniformed officers arrived at her door, with Detective Ota right behind them.

"I heard the address on the scanner," Ota said. "I should've known it was at your place, Ms. Spencer."

On his heels were the crime scene investigation team, with several cases under their arms. They got instructions from Brock on how to proceed.

"I know this looks bad..." she started to say. Instead of finishing, she turned around and put her hands behind her back. "Just handcuff me and take me in for questioning."

"Don't the two of you have a wedding to go to?"

"Well, if we both miss it, maybe no one will notice?" she said.

"I think the bride would notice if you weren't there."

There was the thumping of footsteps coming up the old wooden stairs, and Maile hoped it wasn't the girls being snoopy. Instead, it was Happenstance, leading her 'date' to her room. While that went on, Maile got a text from Lisa:

Where are you? Old lady Stickney is looking tense.
Where's Ronald? Maile texted back.
Hiding in the bathroom. Hurry up.

With nowhere to put it, Maile kept her phone in her hand, expecting more texts.

"What's that all about?" Ota asked, nodding his head at the door that slammed shut at the far end of the hall.

"Can we focus on the kahili over my bed, please?" Maile pled, half for her neighbor's sake.

Brock shared his notes with Ota, and sent the pictures of the stolen items found in Maile's room to him via email. "Am I able to turn this over to you?"

"Yeah, you two get out of here," Ota said. "You have better things to do than hang around a crime scene."

"Does that mean you don't think I'm involved?" Maile asked.

"It means this is all too weird to figure out right now, even for you, Ms. Spencer. It also means I'll have plenty of questions for you later."

"Later today? Or later next week?"

Ota looked at Brock in his tux, and Maile in her gown. He almost seemed to nod a little. "Not today, but don't leave the island."

"I'm not the one going on the honeymoon."

"You know what?" Ota said, looking at her phone in her hand. "I better hang onto your phone."

She held it back from his reach. "Why?"

"I've found in the past, not having your phone helps keep you out of trouble."

"Is this where you tell me it's for my own good?"

"This is where I tell you if you don't hand it over, I take you to the station for questioning and get it from you there." He held his hand out. "All I'm going to do is take a look at the most recent calls and messages. If you have nothing to worry about, that shouldn't be a problem. It would go a long way in determining you had nothing to do with the theft of the kahili or the quilt."

She knew he was right. She also was close enough to the wedding that she no longer needed it that day. It was pretty hard to turn over her lifeline to someone else, though.

"Hand over the phone and you can go to the wedding. Either that or you're coming to the station for questioning."

"Just give him the phone, Maile," Brock said. "If you need to make a call, you can use my phone."

After turning it off, she slapped it in Ota's hand. "Don't erase anything."

Ota slipped it into a small evidence bag and put it in a pocket. "Thanks."

Maile looked at the kahili one last time, the CSI techs finishing the task of dusting for fingerprints along the shafts. "I sure wish I could take those to the church. Lani really had her heart set on finding those in time for the wedding."

Ota went to the techs for a quick discussion. Once he was done, he nodded at them. "Go ahead. They're all yours."

"I can take them? You don't need them for evidence?"

"Sergeant Turner has already gathered photographic evidence, and the evidence boys have collected prints to run." Ota made a point of looking directly at Brock. "I don't see any reason to keep the kahili here, if you promise to take them to the church and nowhere else."

They were joined by someone just coming in.

"Oh, hi, Mrs. Taniguchi. Sorry about all the people in here this morning," Maile said to her landlady. "I know you don't like visitors in our rooms."

"You get my note?"

"Yes."

"You didn't come see me."

"I've been sorta busy. These are police officers, and those things have been stolen. I didn't steal them, though."

"I remember these guys from another time. This stuff is stolen? The feathers and bedspread?"

"Yes, unfortunately," Detective Ota said. He tried stepping between the elderly landlady and Maile, but Mrs. Taniguchi was too quick for him. "Ma'am, do you know anything about these things?"

The old lady nodded slightly. "Let one young guy in here early this morning. Had two friends with him."

Ota flipped open his notebook. "Who were they?"

"Some kind of weird name. Said good friends of Maile, had gifts for her, so I let them in. I watch real careful, too. They never took nothing of hers. Just put those feather things over her bed. The young guy put the bedspread on real careful like, the way a woman would." Mrs. Taniguchi nodded to herself. "Yeah, that's right. He seemed, I don't know, soft."

"Soft?" Ota asked, still writing.

"Like more girl than boy, that kind of soft."

"What else did he look like?"

"Dark skin, but not Polynesian. More like Egyptian. Pretty hair, like he goes to lady's barber all the time. Skinny arms."

"Did he have an accent?"

"Talk English good, but foreign kind way, not like us guys in Hawaii."

"His clothes?"

"Just regular mainland kind. Looked expensive."

"Sounds like Prince Aziz," Maile said under her breath.

"Let me figure that out, and I'd appreciate it without your interference. Are you going to take those things with you or not?" Ota asked.

A door slammed at the far end of the hall, followed by a set of footsteps going down the stairs, and Maile figured Happenstance's date was leaving. She tried reading Mrs. Taniguchi's face, then Ota's, and lastly Brock's. Only Ota seemed concerned, making notes on a fresh page in his little notepad.

All she could do was shrug at Ota when he looked at her for an explanation.

Maile went to one kahili, and Brock went to the other. They were in simple stands and tied together where they crossed over her pillow. After a CSI tech removed the tie and placed that in an evidence bag, Maile and Brock slipped the kahili from their stands. It took some maneuvering to get the heavy tops aimed toward the door in the small room, but they were able to get out to the hallway.

"What about the quilt?" she asked Ota before leaving altogether.

"Probably back to the Iolani Palace by the end of the day."

By the time they had the tall red and yellow kahili down the stairs and out to the sidewalk, the usual breeze had picked up. That fluttered the feathers a little too much, and Maile worried about the artifacts surviving the trip to the church. It wasn't far, but anything could go wrong.

Happenstance was there at the curb, waving to cars passing by. The girls had found her again, and were busy quizzing the hooker about something. Kealoha was watching from a distance.

"Girls!" Maile shouted at the kids, and then thought better of scolding them. "Oh, forget it. Time for them to learn about birds, bees, and Happenstance."

She wondered if Lopaka might have time to come pick them up in the tour van, but he'd have to convince him to go to the tour office, get the van, drive to her place, load the things inside, and then go to the church.

Maybe the best option was to take them back to Detective Ota and the crime scene techs to deal with, and forget about taking them to the church altogether. A hundred things could go wrong in the few miles from her apartment to the church, all of them disastrous in her imagination.

When she saw her mother's face beaming with pride at the sight of the kahili, she knew she had to continue on to the church with them.

"Thérèse, Sammy, go back up to my room and get two big garbage bags for me, please."

The girls hitched up the bottoms of their long muu'muus and made a race of it. Five minutes later, they returned with two bags. While she and Brock held the kahili down at an angle, Kealoha covered the tops with the bags.

When Brock's phone rang, the call was for Maile. He had one of the girls hold it up for her to talk.

"Mai! Why aren't you answering your phone?"

"I guess I left it behind somewhere. What's going on there?"

"Where are you? Lani's freaking out that you and Brock aren't here yet!" Lisa shouted.

"Can't her mother do something?"

"Lei-lei's keeping her busy so she doesn't notice things are hittin' the fan."

"Everything else is okay?" Maile asked.

"That Stickney woman is hiding somewhere."

"Can't Mister Stickney do something about her?"

"We've lost him, too. Not in the bathroom, anyway. I just looked. Can you get here so we can get started before we lose anyone else?"

"Yeah, we have a surprise for everybody. We found the kahili and we're bringing them to the church in a few more minutes."

"Yeah, that's great. The minister needs to start on time because he has another wedding to go to later. What should I do?" Lisa asked.

"Give Mrs. Stickney a pill and a drink when she shows up again. Otherwise, have the chamber quartet play dance music."

"Sounds like trouble?" Brock asked after the call was done.

"Just your average wedding nightmare."

"Not too late to ditch the wedding," he said.

"Don't tempt me."

"The two of you are going to that wedding, and taking these with you," Maile's mother said, now finished with her job of covering the tops of the kahili.

"Just exactly how're we going to do that in your pickup?" Maile asked Brock.

"I just cleaned out the bed yesterday. I don't have any tie-down straps. Somebody will have to sit in the bed and hang on to them."

"Is that even legal?"

"Not really, but I'm a cop and we only have to go a few miles."

"Well, have fun sitting back there."

"Not me, you are," he said. "To make this legit, I need to drive."

"We'll do it!" the girls announced.

"You're not riding in the back of a pickup truck."

"You'll need to, Maile," Brock said.

"Why me? You really think I'm sitting in the bed of a pickup truck in a formal gown, hanging onto kahili as you drive down the street? You know how weird that's going to look?"

"You want your mother to?" he asked.

"No."

He laughed. "It would be a great video to post online. But with me driving, I can get a squad car escort all the way to the church. The extra security would be a good idea."

"Yes, let's bring a little more attention to me riding in the back of your truck in this gown. Sounds great."

He put the tailgate down. "Need help?"

"Maybe you can give me a boost?"

Maile heard phone cameras clicking as Brock boosted her up, giving her bottom one last push. When she looked down, she saw her mother and both girls busy taking pictures with their phones.

"If I see even one of those on anyone's Facebook, you're all in trouble!"

All three giggled as they got in the pickup along with Brock. When the police car escort got there, they started slowly, allowing Maile to find a stable position. Her hair whipped about in the wind, and the taffeta fabric on her gown fluttered, hinting at the possibility of a Marilyn Monroe type of wardrobe malfunction from the waist down. That wasn't as bad as the honks and catcalls she got from other drivers. When they got to the church and parked, Brock lifted Maile down from the tailgate.

"Seriously, never doing that again," she said. A couple of the groomsmen had come out and were waiting. She handed over the kahili to the men she knew were trustworthy, and left them to take the feathered standards into the church.

Hurrying with the kids, she led them to the front entrance of the church.

"Okay, I need to go find my friends and get fixed up. The two of you stay with my mom, got it? Turn off your phones and please sit still during the ceremony."

"Their mothers are here already," Kealoha said. "They both got calls while we were waiting on the sidewalk.

"Here at the church?"

"Came straight here from the airport. Probably waiting inside."

Maile put her hands up in surrender. "My watch is done. I release you to your mothers! Go and be one with your families!"

Both girls hitched up their muu'muus and trotted up the stairs.

"See ya, Maile!"

"Bye!"

Maile couldn't help but smile at the adventure she'd had with them. "Mom, where are you sitting? They have a special pew set up for you."

"I'm not sitting in the queen's pew. That's for you someday, when we finally get Hawaii back."

"Please don't push an agenda today. I'm too exhausted for that."

Kealoha waved Maile away. "Go, be with your friends. I'll find a place to sit."

"Maybe Reverend Ka'uhane is waiting?"

Kealoha waved as she went up the steps. Maile peeked in the door and saw the matching kahili in their rightful places, standing tall and proud, no trace of their adventures outside, or of the garbage bags. With a longer look, she noticed Mrs. Fortuna seated on the bride's side of the long aisle, but couldn't see Mr. Fortuna. There were too many people standing around at the front chatting, that she couldn't see what Mrs. Stickney might've been doing, and wouldn't know her husband to recognize him.

She spotted the two girls sitting with their mothers. Thérèse was cheerfully waving her arms about, recalling the events of the last day or so, and Samantha sat rigid as she got a silent scolding from her mother. Lopaka was there with his wife, both dressed in the nicest aloha attire the island had to offer. She recognized several others from church, the hospital, the Manoa House meetings, and even from other islands. The rest of the large nave was full of well-dressed people from every walk of life Honolulu had to offer. Lani would have the big day she had been hoping for.

"Okay, time to go have a wedding."

Keepers of the Kingdom

Chapter Eleven

There was a small building about the size of a house just across the driveway from the church steps. It housed a small office, kitchen, and most importantly a meeting room that bridal parties could use as a place for last minute preparations. When she went in, she found Lani being primped over by the other bridesmaids, and Lisa busy taking pictures of Lani's last moments as 'a free woman'. A bottle of white wine had been opened but sat ignored on a table, surrounded by empty glasses. The atmosphere wasn't nearly as dramatic as what she'd feared.

Lei-lei was there, positioned to ambush Maile when she came in. She gave her a hug.

"I'm never doing this again," Lei-lei whispered.

"Either am I. Sorry I'm late. Everything looked okay in the church. How're things in here?"

"Only minor panic attacks and emotional mayhem," Jenn, one of the bridesmaids said.

"I heard you found the kahili?" Lani asked Maile. "Where were they?"

"Long story. Basically, in storage. I just looked and they're right where they belong behind the altar."

"Everything's ready," Lisa said, now taking video on her phone. "Just need to take that long walk down the aisle."

"Last chance to skip out, Lani!" Maile said, as Jenn went about the task of fixing her hair into a fancy twist.

"Yeah, any last minute doubts?" Lisa asked, laughing.

"About a hundred of them, just in the last five minutes!" Lani said. The finishing touch, the veil was draped over her face. "Just don't let me near that door alone, or I might bolt!"

Maile's updo was being lacquered in place with hair spray when there was a knock at the door. A man in a tuxedo looked in.

"Dad!" Lani shouted. "Come in!"

Mr. Fortuna had emotions written all over his face. Maile's father had passed long before her own wedding, and she'd always wondered how he would've behaved in that moment. Her heart and her eyes were both close to bursting when she saw him.

"It looks like everyone is here now," he said, looking at Maile. Jenn was stabbing tiny flowers into her stiff hair, using shots of spray to glue them in place.

"We're ready to go!" Lani said. "I'd give you a hug, but I can't risk messing up this dress, or veil, or anything else."

"You look wonderful, Daughter. I've never seen someone so beautiful."

"Since Mom was your bride," Lani said. Even with the heavy makeup, Maile could tell she was blushing.

"Is it time?" Lisa asked, still filming what was going on in the room.

"Not quite yet. I should have a talk with my daughter."

"Uh oh! Last minute talk with Dad!" Lisa said, still aiming her phone at them.

"Hate to break it to you, Mister Fortuna, but Lani already knows what to expect on the honeymoon!" Jenn said. She gave Maile's hair one last blast of spray.

The other bridesmaids hushed to silence. Maile could tell something more important was coming than simple well wishes from a father.

Mr. Fortuna poured five glasses of wine and handed them to each bridesmaid, keeping one in his hand for his daughter. When he led Lani off to one corner to talk privately, Maile positioned herself to try and eavesdrop. She hadn't had the benefit of getting the same talk on her big day.

It sounded as though it started as a pep talk, but changed into something about Ronald and Mrs. Stickney.

"Where is he?" Lani demanded suddenly. "He's still in the bathroom? Get that idiot in the church!"

"Uh oh," Lisa said, giggling. She raised her phone to take a secret video of Lani. "First marital spat and they haven't been to the altar yet."

Maile put her hand over the phone. "Maybe not a good idea right now."

That's when Lani, still in the corner with her father, blotted a tear at the corner of her eye. She was just as angry as she was distraught. If it were on social media, it would be hilarious, with a beautiful bride in an elegant gown and veil having a meltdown. Right then, in that room, no one was laughing as Mr. Fortuna ended his message.

"Where are they? Get them in here!"

Maile and the others went to where Mr. Fortuna was trying to settle his daughter. "What's going on?" Lisa asked.

"That idiot…" That's when Lani's face exploded into tears. "Get him in here…now!"

"I don't understand," Maile said.

"Where's Ronald?" Jenn asked.

"Mister Stickney just had a talk with me. It sounds like Ronald has had second thoughts."

"About getting married today?" Maile asked.

"About getting married at all."

"What the..." Lisa started to say. She finally lowered her camera.

Maile was pissed, not just for Lani, but for all of them to have gone through so many efforts to arrange such a big event, and for the costs the Fortunas had paid to make it all happen. She wanted blood as much as Lani must've wanted to hide. "Where's Ronald? I want to talk to him."

"From what I understand, he's on his way to the airport."

"He left me?" Lani looked up from under her veil. When she tried drying her face through it, she pulled it free from her head and flung it away. "Where'd he go? Is he already on the honeymoon, waiting for me? Is this a gag? Because this is not funny!"

"He went home, Honey. With his mother."

"When?" Lani looked unsteady. "Maybe I can catch him at the airport?"

"An hour or so ago. I guess there was too much of a delay."

The biggest pang of guilt Maile had ever felt hit her square in the heart. She wanted to argue that she got to the church well before noon, the scheduled start time, but right then wasn't the time.

"Mister Stickney only stayed behind to let us know..."

When Lani dropped, she hit the floor like a sack of potatoes. Maile was first at her side, followed by Mr. Fortuna and Lei-lei. Lisa and the others were having meltdowns of their own. At one point while trying to pull Lani from her fainting spell, Maile heard a wine bottle get uncorked.

Once they had Lani up and into a chair with a full glass of wine in her hand, Lisa and Jenn took Maile aside.

"She's a wreck," Lisa whispered.

"No kidding," Maile whispered back.

Jenn nodded at Lani still being comforted by her father. Her color looked too pale for life, and her dark eyes stared straight ahead. "Look. She's going sideways with this. You need to go take care of her, Mai."

"Me? Why me? That's the maid of honor's job."

"You're the nurse. You know what to say," Lisa said.

"Lei's already with her."

"Okay, fine. I'll stay here with them while the two of you go tell everyone in the church the wedding's off. Including Mrs. Fortuna."

Lisa and Jenn shook their heads. "Forget that. I'm not going in there with them, not with that message."

"I'm not sending her father in there. He needs to be with her right now. Where's the best man?"

"Derek? He'd make a mess of it. Maybe Brock…"

"I'm not sticking him with it." Maile poured a glass of wine and drank it all in one long gulp. "I'll go. But get Lani in her dad's car with him and out of here. She's doesn't deserve any more of a scene than what this has already become."

With a kiss to her cheek and a squeeze of Lani's hand, Maile left the tragedy behind. Going up the church steps, she wondered what sort of drama was coming next. As she walked down the aisle, the bridal march was started by the quartet, and everyone watched her intently as she went toward the altar. Once she got there, the music abruptly stopped. She shook her head slightly as a signal to Reverend Akamu that the wedding was off. She found Mrs. Fortuna still sitting alone in the front pew. She held the woman's hand as she explained what she knew.

"I'm very sorry. We're all terribly disappointed."

"I wondered if something was going wrong last night during that party. That Stickney woman just isn't a happy person." Mrs. Fortuna gently, almost calmly blew her nose. "I guess I should make some sort of announcement."

"Actually, your husband already has Lani in the car out front and is waiting for you. I can tell the others."

Maile watched as the woman made her way down the aisle to the door, nodding politely to friends in the pews. Once she was gone, Maile went to the front. She tried smiling but failed miserably.

"Yes, well, thank you everyone for being here today. As you can see, two very important participants aren't here." She gritted her teeth against the tension in her voice. "Lani and Ronald have decided that today won't be their big day after all."

After answering a few questions, Maile made her own jailbreak for a side door. Reverend Akamu was there to offer a few words of comfort, which she accepted while barely slowing down. Brock met her just outside, waiting in the sunshine. He was just ending a call and putting his phone away.

"I didn't think this was coming off today," he said.

"Neither did I. I bet that Stickney woman had more to do with it than Ronald simply having cold feet."

"Are you going to the reception?"

"Can't think of a grimmer place to be than at a wedding reception with no bride or groom. Anyway, I've given up on the whole thing. I just want to go home and get out of this dress. Want to meet later?" she asked.

"Um, well, you see..." He acted like a little kid, wondering how to apologize to a parent for breaking a window. "...I just made a date to meet someone."

Maile felt the blood drain from her face for the second time in less than an hour. "Someone?"

"Yeah, I have a...I'm meeting..."

Maile's molars clamped together. "You just made a date with someone? I thought I was supposed to be your date today?"

"We never made any plans for later, Maile. There's nothing exclusive between us. You know that."

When Maile turned to leave, she left a few choice words floating in the air behind her.

"You have a way to get home?" Brock called after her. "You don't even have your phone or wallet."

"I have my bus pass."

"In that dress? Where?"

She turned around to face him. Crossing her arms over her chest created a little more cleavage. "You want to search me for it? Because you'll have to take me on a date first."

By the time she got to the front entrance to the church grounds, the Fortunas were gone, and the other bridesmaids were nowhere to be found.

"Probably in a bar, which is exactly where I should be."

Maile needed to walk two blocks to get to a stop for a bus that would take her home. She knew she looked peculiar crossing streets with her heavy makeup, stiff hair, and elegant taffeta gown. She almost felt as though she were making a weird pop music video of some sort, and someone had forgotten to play the sad song that went with it.

She was getting a close inspection by a homeless man when her bus arrived. She was the third person to get on, and felt something on her rear as she passed by the man. She aimed an acrylic fingernail at his face. "Don't even start."

She had to gather her gown as she climbed the steps into the bus.

"Where's the groom?" the young Samoan bus driver asked when Maile flashed her bus pass.

"Turns out marriage is easier without the man."

He pulled into traffic after Maile sat in the handicap seat right behind him. "That include me?"

"I'm too tired and too angry for any man to want to deal with me today."

As he drove, Maile told the story of the wedding that didn't quite happen.

"Oh, yeah," the driver said. "That guy needs some trouble to find him."

"And his mother. I think when karma finds them, it ain't gonna be pretty."

He brought the bus to a stop on her block. "Good luck to your friend. I hope she meets a nicer guy next time."

"Let's hope there is a next time."

"Eh, why you riding the bus home? No handsome man in a tuxedo at that church?"

"Better fish in the sea, as they say."

There were still two police cars and a crime scene evidence van parked in front of her apartment building. The sight of them drained the last ounce of energy from Maile. All she wanted to do was fall into bed and sleep the rest of the day. The worst news of all was that Detective Ota's sedan was still parked there. Checking the time on her watch, she saw barely two hours had passed since leaving there in the morning with the kahili in Brock's truck.

Walking down the sidewalk toward the front door of the building, Maile tried to decide on what to do. She could ride the buses for the day, but knew she'd have to fend off pickup artists at every stop. She could go to her mother's cottage, but would face a game of twenty questions of why didn't she see Lani's trouble coming. With only a bus pass, her phone in Ota's pocket, and her keys in Brock's truck, all she could really do was go home and try to get rid of Ota and his troop of uniforms.

A car pulled to the curb and out got Rosamie, bringing several grocery bags with her. When she was spotted by her neighbor, Maile went over to help carry bags.

"Home from the wedding? Still got time before the reception?" her neighbor asked and they lugged bags into the building.

"Wedding called off. I'm sure someone is drinking booze at a reception for a bride and groom who have gone into hiding. Which is exactly where I should be, if I had any money."

"Bride got cold feet?"

"Groom."

"Men are dogs. Did he find out her dad's loading up the shotgun?"

"What? No, she's not pregnant. At least, not that I know of."

"Hey, speaking of shotguns, I still need to talk to you about something."

"Can it wait till tomorrow?" Maile asked. She saw Mrs. Taniguchi, their landlady standing near the stairs, her arms folded, one foot tapping impatiently on the floor. She didn't look happy.

"Till after church?" Rosamie asked.

"Till after I sober up." She tried smiling at Mrs. Taniguchi as they approached the woman's gauntlet of glares.

"Miss Spencer, why are there so many men in your room?"

"They're police, right?"

"There are five of them."

"I'm sorry, Mrs. Taniguchi. I'll do my best to get rid of them," Maile said, as she and Rosamie went up the creaking wooden stairs.

The elderly landlady followed after. "You know the house rules. Entertaining only during the daytime, and only one at a time."

"I'm not entertaining them. They're police officers investigating a crime."

"Why the police here? What crime?"

"You saw them morning. Did you check with the detective in my room about anything new?"

"Detective in your room!" Mrs. Taniguchi stopped partway up. "I thought you were a good girl when I let you have that room!" After a brief rest, Mrs. Taniguchi kept following them. "All the time the police coming around. Trouble, that's your name. No more good girls in this town."

"Maybe I can join Happenstance on the sidewalk? Happenstance and Trouble, wayward sistahs of the evening."

Rosamie giggled. "Happenstance has been busy today."

Seeing her door hanging open and hearing several voices all talking at once over police work and evidence matters, Maile took bags into Rosamie's apartment hoping to hide.

"Wanna stay in here?" the neighbor offered in a whisper.

"I need to go face the music. They've gotta be done pretty soon." There was a knock at Rosamie's door. Maile sighed. "Probably for me."

Detective Ota was standing at the door when Maile opened it. A uniformed police officer was there with him.

"Ms. Spencer. I'd like a word with you."

"Are you guys almost done? Because I really need to change clothes and some peace and quiet."

Neither Ota nor the officer budged as she tried to cross the hall to her own apartment. "You can get that downtown." He nodded at the officer.

The officer pulled handcuffs from his belt. "Maile Spencer, you're under arrest. Anything you say can and will be used against you in…"

Chapter Twelve

"What's going on?" she asked, looking at the cuffs in the cop's hand.

"Ma'am, please turn around so I can put these on," the officer said.

Maile turned most of the way around to feel cold steel get clasped around her wrists. Rosamie was watching from inside her apartment. Her husband arrived just then and ducked past them to join Rosamie. Maybe most humiliating right then was being arrested right in front of Mrs. Taniguchi.

"What am I being arrested for?" she asked Ota, who looked genuinely unhappy about what was happening right then.

"Breaking and entering a museum on federal land, grand theft of a priceless artifact, breaking and entering a place of worship, and grand theft of church property."

"You're arresting me for the quilt and kahili?"

"Yes, Ma'am," the officer said.

"You got all that from my phone? Because there's nothing in there that can incriminate me."

"I haven't had the chance to look at your phone. I've been busy with something else," Ota said.

"Should've figured this was coming." She yanked at her wrists cuffed behind her back. "I have to wear these?"

"Not much choice, Ma'am."

"Can I at least change my clothes before you take me in?"

"Your entire apartment is a crime scene and needs to be processed by my techs," Ota said.

"Seriously? I have to wear a bridesmaid dress to the police station?"

"Not much choice."

When Ota reached for her arm to lead her away, Mrs. Taniguchi got in his way.

"Where you take my girl?" the old lady asked Ota, craning her neck to look up at him. "Second time today you make trouble for my tenants."

"Downtown police station for questioning." He reached for Maile again. "Please…"

"Maile's a good girl. Never any trouble. You leave her be."

"I need to…" He reached for Maile's arm and pulled her forward past Mrs. Taniguchi. "She needs to come with me."

"What's your name?"

"Detective David Ota, of the Honolulu Police Department." He gave her a business card.

Mrs. Taniguchi squeezed the card into her hand. "You that Ota boy I know from Mo'ili'ili Hongwanji?"

"No, I don't think so. Sorry."

The old lady continued to block their way while she took off the ever-present sweater she wore. "Maile no can go to prison like that. You wear my sweater."

Maile couldn't figure the quick change in the woman's attitude toward her right then, but left that for another time. "Thanks, but they'll just take it from me at the jail."

With Detective Ota leading Maile to the stairs, she in her gown and handcuffs, and him in a sports coat and slacks, they left behind their audience of police officers, Rosamie and her husband, and Mrs. Taniguchi.

"If you're the Ota boy I remember, I'm calling your mother about this," Mrs. Taniguchi called to them.

Halfway down the stairs, he looked at Maile. "She's tough."

"You have no idea."

"She's serious about calling my mother?"

"She's probably already looking in the phone book and will spend the rest of the day calling every Ota she can find." She rattled the cuffs behind her back again. "What a sight I must be. Bridesmaid in handcuffs. You really had to do that in front of my friends?"

"Not much choice. I don't like audiences for that sort of thing any more than you do."

"Why can't I change into other clothes?"

"To preserve the scene for evidence collection. It's as much for your protection as it is for anything procedural." Opening the rear passenger door for her, he set his hand on the top of her head as she sat and pivoted in. Once he was behind the steering wheel and out in traffic, he looked at her in his rearview mirror. "How was the wedding?"

"Didn't happen," she said, looking out the window at the familiar landscape.

"I thought you got home a little early. Where's Brock?"

"That's what I'd like to know." They came to the intersection with McCully, a busy place in central Honolulu. She looked off in one direction near a building decorated fancifully in red and yellow. "May I ask a favor?"

"Need a meal?"

"I haven't eaten since breakfast yesterday."

"Chinese okay?"

"I was hoping you'd offer that. Chop Suey City?"

He made a hard right turn when the signal changed. Five minutes later, they parked in front of a Chinese restaurant that was frequented by police officers for on-duty meals. He helped her out of the car.

"Are you taking these off, or what?" she asked, rattling her cuffs.

"Inside. And don't try running, because there're others in there that can chase you down dressed like that."

"This dress wouldn't slow me down much, but I'm not looking to escape. There's something else I need to know."

"What's that?" he asked, taking the cuffs off her in the waiting area inside.

She rubbed her wrists. "Nothing you need to worry about."

A young waitress in an emerald green cheongsam led them to a large table in a back corner of the restaurant, the usual place for police officers to eat. The whole way, she kept glancing at the gown Maile was wearing. By the time Maile was seated between two officers, the waitress had a disapproving look to her face when she handed Maile a menu.

The waitress wasn't the usual one she saw there. Instead, she looked like a younger, skinnier sister of Miss Wong, who she was hoping to find.

"Excuse me. Is Miss Wong here today?" Maile asked.

"Day off for her."

"You know where she is?"

"Why you care about her so much?"

"Just that she's always here."

"Wong's got a date."

"You know with who?" Maile asked.

The waitress scanned the men at the table, who were all very intently looking down at their plates of food. "Don't know. We serve food here, not girls."

"Bring me two orders of spring rolls, and not leftovers from yesterday."

The waitress hurried away with Maile's order.

Maile looked at the table of officers with her. Instead of their usual banter and police talk, they barely said anything at all, not even about her clothing or fancy makeup and hairdo. "Brock been here in the last few minutes?" she asked anyone that might answer.

"Brock?" one of them asked, acting innocent.

"Yeah, Sergeant Brock Turner. You must know him."

"Haven't seen him."

"Me neither," another said.

"I thought he had a wedding to go to today?"

"And a reception," Maile said. "Any of you know who he was meeting after it?"

"I would've guessed you," Ota said. He noticed the others suddenly look at him, worry on their faces. "Did I miss something?"

Like a troupe of synchronized acrobats doing a performance, all four uniformed officers tossed money down on the table to pay for their meals and bolted for the door.

"I think both of us missed something," Maile said. She ate quickly when her meal came, now that her question about Brock had been answered. "You can't interrogate me here? We really have to go to the station?"

"It needs to be a formal questioning. It really is in…"

"Yes, I know. It's in my best interest that you parade me around in this costume when I'm dead tired and cranky." She looked up at him while dunking her spring roll into a bowl of sauce. "Wait. Was someone murdered?"

"Not today. But now that you bring it up, I doubt it'll be long before someone drops dead in your presence."

Maile bit the spring roll in half and chewed. "If that good for nothing groom showed up in here right now, there might be a homicide."

While packing away one last spring roll, Maile told the story of how the groom went home with his mother, leaving Maile's friend at the altar.

"Almost literally at the altar. She was ready to walk down the aisle when we got the word he skipped out on her."

"What did Brock have to say?" Ota asked.

"That he had a date with someone else this afternoon."

"Ouch."

"No kidding."

"What did he have to say about the wedding being called off?" Ota asked.

"Oh, that. Everybody in the church was as surprised as Lani was. I should give her a call, but I don't have my phone, which is in your pocket."

"It's safe and sound locked in my desk at the station."

"You've already been to the station and back to my apartment? Why'd you go in and come back so fast?"

"Your friend, Miss Happenstance performed a little too much business that I couldn't ignore."

"So, you arrested her? It's like you got a two-fer at my apartment building," she said.

"That was the business that I couldn't ignore."

Ota put some money on the table to pay for their meals. In the small waiting area at the front, she turned around so he could put the handcuffs back on.

"I'll pay you back for the meal," she said. "It was my idea to come here."

"You wanted to come just to see if the usual waitress was here?"

"You're not the only one who can do an investigation, Detective."

"Did you really need to interrogate the waitress that was here, though?"

"I got what I needed, didn't I? I learned that from you."

"I still wish you'd consider a career in law enforcement," he said, helping her into the back of his sedan.

"I already seem to have one, just from the wrong side of the cuffs." At the police station, he led her past the booking station, good news for her. Maybe there wasn't too much trouble after all, and she could get out of there after answering a few questions. The bad news was that she was the center of attention being dressed the way she was at a police station. Prostitutes came and went in police stations, but not bridesmaids. As thin and frumpy as Mrs. Taniguchi's sweater was, Maile wished she'd accepted it, just to cover some exposed skin. "Okay, why am I here? Why couldn't this have been done somewhere else?"

"A number of reasons, and yes, it really is best that we discuss things here. First, you need to know that the fingerprints found on the staffs of the kahili belong to only one person. Guess who?"

"Since you just removed handcuffs, I have to guess me?"

"I've been beating myself over the head trying to think of some way your fingerprints got on stolen property and no one else's. Any ideas?"

"Not a clue, sorry."

"You never handled the kahili until after I released them this morning?"

"Not at all. Not until we found them in my room. Brock...Officer Turner was there at the time. I would think he'd be a reliable eyewitness to the events of this morning."

He poised a pencil on a yellow pad, ready to write. "Relate them to me again, everything that happened before I arrived."

"I was at my mother's cottage in Manoa. You know where that's at. You spend as much time there as I do lately. Even though I was already dressed for the wedding, I needed to drive from there to my apartment to get a necklace to wear for the ceremony. When I went out to it, my car wouldn't start, even after several tries. My mother and the two kids that were with me at the time should be able to corroborate that. Running short on time, and dressed the way I was, I decided against calling for a taxi or taking the bus. I called Brock Turner for a ride, since he was going to the wedding also.

"He arrived a few minutes later in his quad cab-style pickup truck, and gave the two girls, my mother, and me a ride to my apartment. The only reason I needed to go there was for the necklace. But, my mother insisted on seeing the inside of my place since she'd never visited before. The two girls were also curious, and the entire group went up with me. When I unlocked the door…"

"You used all the locks on the door?" he asked. "There are several."

"Yes, every time I go in or out, just like you've suggested several times. The locks were installed by a handyman that I found at the hardware store when I bought the locks. I now have the sturdiest doorframe in the building, but it would be easy to push through the thin door anyway."

"How long ago did you get them installed?" he asked.

"Two weeks ago today."

"Separate keys for each of the locks?"

"The doorknob and one deadbolt are the same. The other two deadbolts have different keys. There are also two sliding bolts to use for when I'm inside, along with a chain. Honestly, I don't see how any of them are keeping me safe if someone was able to get past them to put those kahili and the quilt inside my room."

Ota waved at her to calm down. "Enough about the doors and locks. Tell me about what happened after you opened the door."

"I swung the door open and..."

"Where were the others at the time you opened the door?"

"My mother was to my left and the girls were to my right. We needed to jockey for position to determine who went in first."

"Where was Turner?" Ota asked.

"Right behind me. Since he's several inches taller than me, and a foot taller than my mom and the girls, he should've had no problem seeing over our heads."

"Who went in first?"

"I took a step and stopped. That's when Brock...whatever, must've noticed the kahili and quilt, because he told me to stop and kept the others in the hall. Unfortunately, both of those little girls are very nosy and got in before I could hold them back."

"Did they touch anything?" he asked.

"Maybe the quilt for only a moment. They never got close to the kahili that I saw."

"That you saw." He turned a page on his yellow pad. "What about your mother?"

"She looked at one corner of the quilt, at the stitching, and determined it was authentic. Mostly, she just stood still after that, making the rest of us go around her. She's getting good at that these last few years."

"What was Turner doing when all this was taking place?"

"Taking pictures with his phone, and calling for a police car for back-up, and an evidence team."

"Why did he call for back up?"

"I don't know. Maybe because he was off-duty and needed to go to the wedding? That's your business, not mine."

"Okay, was anybody else in the apartment at the time?"

"What? No, of course not."

"Did you let anyone use your apartment during that night?"

"Of course not. It's not exactly luxury B and B digs at the Coconut Palms Apartments and Refugee Center."

"Please try to remain serious about this, Ms. Spencer."

Maile took a deep breath. "Okay, fine. No, I allowed no one to use my apartment yesterday, or at any other time that I've been a resident in that building. No one lives there with me, no one has ever stayed over, I've slept alone every night I've been there."

He glanced up at her over his half-glasses. "Thank you for clarifying that with supportive detail. Who else has access to your apartment?"

"As in who has keys? Rosamie across the hall has a set, as does Mrs. Taniguchi. They were both there when you arrested me a while ago. Watching. You know, when the officer put handcuffs on me and read me my rights."

"I remember. I still need to talk with them."

"Please don't arrest Rosamie in front of her kids, and don't muscle Mrs. Taniguchi around too much. She's twice as old as you and weighs about as much as a sheet of paper."

"I'm not going to muscle anyone around. I just need to verify with them they let no one into your apartment last night or this morning."

"Mrs. Taniguchi let someone in early this morning, but she couldn't remember his name. Brock...Sergeant Turner has that information in his little notepad book thingie."

"Good." He flipped to the new, blank page. "Now, back to the matter of your fingerprints being on the two poles. Any ideas about that?"

"No clue. For as many times as I've been in the Kawaiaha'o Church, I've never once handled those kahili."

"Not till this morning."

"Right. And you were the one who gave me permission to do so. Sergeant Turner was there at the time, and assisted me with carrying them to his truck for transport to the church."

"Thank you for reminding me. What handyman did you use for the locks?"

"I have his card at home, and his number would be stored in my phone, which is in your drawer. Otherwise, his name was Jeff Bedford. Something like that."

"What'd he look like?"

"Maybe not quite six foot, dark hair, athletic but not big. In his thirties. Wore a long sleeve blue and red plaid shirt over a white T-shirt, and jeans."

"How do you remember so much detail if it was two weeks ago?"

"Nobody wears jeans and long sleeved flannel over a T-shirt in the tropics, unless they're new here or trying to sweat off a few pounds in a hurry. I don't remember his face so well, but his clothes made an impression."

"Anything else about him?"

"Maybe I'm being a little judgmental, but he seemed especially well-groomed for a handyman."

Ota began writing again. "How so?"

"His clothes smelled freshly laundered as though he used fabric softener, he was neatly groomed, freshly shaven, tidy haircut. Clean nails."

"How is that judgmental?"

"I guess I've always expected a handyman to have dirty hands from doing work. I dunno."

"He didn't have sawdust all over him from cutting lumber?" Ota asked, still writing.

Feeling her cheeks flush red with embarrassment, Maile sat back in her chair. "Not that I noticed."

"Check his license?"

"What's his driver's license got to do with installing locks on my door? I had no reason to question his identity. He did a quick and easy cash job for me, and that was the end of it."

"His business license."

"Someone needs a business license to be a handyman?" she asked.

"In this city, they do. This is the exact reason why, too. When something like this happens, I need to trace down everybody that may have had access to a crime scene, before and during the time of the criminal act. If he's licensed, bonded, and insured, it goes a long way in verifying his legitimacy, and in eliminating him as a suspect."

"Next time, I'll ask. I promise."

"What hardware store?"

"Matsui Hardware and Nursery in Manoa, not far from my mother's cottage."

"I know the place." Using his desk phone, he made a quick call, using mostly police jargon. After the call, he went behind her like a gentleman to help scoot the chair back.

"You're taking me home? I don't have to ride the bus across downtown looking like this?"

"Visiting the cellblock for a while."

Chapter Thirteen

Maile couldn't figure why Detective Ota was being so polite right before locking her in a cell. "Cellblock? Why?"

"I need to go talk to a few people, including your landlady and neighbor. Then I need to track down that handyman."

"His number is in my phone."

"Just so you know, and please don't have a fit, but I had a cursory look in your phone and checked a few of the new numbers. The number you have in there for Jeff Bedford is no longer active. That means a trip to the hardware store to see if they know anything about him. While I do that, you're waiting in a cell. I should put your necklace in my desk."

She took it off. "It's paste, not worth much."

"It's trouble in a cellblock." He looked at it closely. "You're sure this is paste?"

"The Fortunas wouldn't hand out real stuff, would they?"

"If they're wealthy enough, and it sounds like that are, they'd give the bridesmaids a gift."

When he put it his desk drawer, she noticed her phone and keys in there. "How'd you learn about Jeff Bedford so fast?"

"That's the part that you're not supposed to have a fit about. His was one of the more recent new numbers in your call log, something that's suspicious to police. Believe it or not, I'm trying to use your phone to help you. But since that number is no longer active, I need to go talk to the people at the hardware store to see if they know anything about him."

He led her to the door that entered into the cellblock.

"You're going to go lean on old man Matsui? I think you'll find he's just as tough as Mrs. Taniguchi."

"Not going to lean on anybody," Ota said.

She went through the electronically locked security door into the cellblock first. The cellblock guard led her from there, a large set of keys in his hand.

"But why do I have to sit in a cell?"

"This is going to take me a few hours, and I don't have anywhere else to put you."

"Home wouldn't be so bad."

"Still a crime scene, and before you suggest your mother's place, that needs to be off limits to you for a day or two."

Being led out by another officer was a tall woman in leopard print tights and a tube top. Maile needed a second glance to realize it was Happenstance being let out of jail while she was on her way in. Maile did her best to turn her face away as they went past each other.

"You really brought her in?" Maile asked Ota, once Happenstance was gone.

"She could've been more discreet, especially when there are so many cops around."

The guard stopped at a cell full of women in various types of clothing. None of them were happy, and all demanded to see their lawyers. There was a greater intensity of anguish than usual.

As always, the sliding cell door slammed shut as soon as Maile was inside. And also as always, she was facing several other women, all of them but one looking as tough as linebackers in petit hooker outfits. Only other woman was by herself, dressed more like a housewife, looking a little bleary-eyed. The cellblock bar she clung to seemed to be the only thing holding her up right then.

A petit Asian woman about Maile's age pushed her way through the group. She was dressed in a black tube top with separate long sleeves, black hot pants, and black fishnet hose. She looked to be sporting a fat lip. Suzie Suzuki was familiar to Maile, unfortunately. Wavy black hair hung in every direction from her head, nearly hiding her face. Her heavily made-up face was the exact opposite in how Maile's face was made up.

"Well, lookey who we have here! What'd Ota do, raid a wedding?"

Maile turned around to ignore her and tried making eye contact with the drunk housewife in the corner.

"Hey! I'm talking to you, Bridal Babe!"

Maile felt several pairs of eyes trained on her.

"Don't call me that." Seeing the lonely woman in the corner close up for the first time, she had a black eye. Maile went closer to the housewife. She got a whiff of the booze that had caused the trouble for the woman. "You okay?"

"No. They're mean."

"Not exactly the cream of Honolulu society in here. What're you in for? Drunk driving?"

"More like plastered driving."

"Get the black eye from an accident or from them?" Maile asked.

"Them." The woman wavered a little just lifting her head to look at Maile. "They're mean."

"You said that already. Maybe you should sit down before you fall down?"

"Where? Nowhere to sit except on the pot, and that's how I got this," the housewife said, pointing a shaky finger at her face.

"Suit yourself. All I know if that the floor is a lot softer with a planned landing."

Maile felt a tapping in her shoulder. When she turned around, she came face to face with Suzie. Several others were right behind her, more of Honolulu's curbside finest.

"Nobody walks away from me, Bridesmaid. Especially not you."

Maile tried to get closer, but there was no space to step into. "First time for everything, even for someone with as much experience as you."

"What's that supposed to mean?"

"It means whatever you want it to mean."

Suzie's face twisted with confusion for a moment before snapping back to a glare. "What're you all dressed up for, anyway? Making money at church socials these days?"

"Seriously…" Maile leaned in close, almost touching noses with Suzie. "…back off."

"Make me."

"Yeah! Make her, Bridesmaid!" someone said.

Maile was in a spot. She felt like taking a swing or two at Suzie, but that would lead to a wrestling match, which she'd won in the past. On the other hand, she'd bought the gown for a stiff price and had plans to re-use it in the future. The fight she really felt like having right then would only split seams and crumple taffeta.

Maile postured with her hands on her hips. She wasn't going to be baited into a fight. Not this time. "I thought I've done that a couple times already, right here in this very same cell?"

Suzie's eyelid ticked nervously. "I'm not afraid of you."

"Then you have no problem walking away."

"I'm not walking away, either."

"Okay, fine. Stand there and stare at me like an idiot."

"You callin' me an idiot?" Suzie asked.

"Seems to fit."

"Just be careful, Bridesmaid. That pretty face of yours might not last until your boyfriend Ota comes back for you." Suzie turned around and started to walk away.

"At least my dates speak in complete sentences. The only sentences you know about are served in here."

When Suzie spun around, she swung a hand. Maile was able to back away in time, getting only a fingernail across a cheek. It took only nanoseconds before her hand swung back, catching her cellblock nemesis square in the chops. The next thing she knew was that she was rolling around on the floor locked in battle. That's when the hooting and hollering started with the other women, cheering on their favorite contenders.

Suzie got a hand into Maile's stiff hairdo and yanked back, while Maile tried rolling over and getting on top of the smaller woman. Once she was straddled on Suzie's hips, but her hair still clutched in a hand and pulling her head around, she pushed down on Suzie's shoulders, pinning her to the floor.

The electronic door buzzed and opened, the guard coming through. He seemed completely unconcerned about the fight that was being waged in the middle of the cell floor.

"Suzuki, you're out! You made bail!"

"Get off me, witch!" Suzie shouted, while swinging her free arm wildly. One swing caught Maile on the chin, rattling her teeth a little.

"Don't call me that!"

As skinny as she was, Suzie found a way of shinnying from beneath Maile. When she stood, something was missing. She held both her hands to her head.

"Hey! Gimme my hair!"

Maile looked at what was in her hand. It was a black wig, the total hairstyle pulled from Suzie's head. Scrambling to her feet, she saw what was bothering Suzie so much. "What happened to your head?"

"I shaved it, okay? It was coming out. You pulled some of it out last time you were here, remember? Now, gimme my hair!"

That's when Maile remembered their last meeting about a month before. She wanted to laugh at the girl, with half-inch long black hair flat to her scalp. As it was, she knew her style was hanging off to one side in a mangled knot. "Not till you promise to lay off other people in here."

"Forget it! They make trouble with me!"

Maile hid the wig behind her back. "Okay, fine. I'm keeping your hair."

"Hey, Suzuki!" the guard shouted. "You want out or not?"

"Not till I get my hair!"

"Have it your way. I don't care if you're in or out. You'll be back in here tomorrow anyway."

With one hand on her hip, Suzie stuck out her other hand in a silent demand for the wig. In her hand was a gardenia bud that had been pulled from Maile's hairdo. Maile knew that the fights would stop if Suzie was released, the only reason she tossed the wig back to her.

Suzie tossed the flower bud back. "There's your stupid flower."

"Have a nice night in Chinatown," Maile hissed as Suzie left the cell.

"Have fun at your wedding, Bridesmaid."

Once the cell was locked and Suzie was gone, the rest of the women went their separate ways, after leaving Maile with one last warning glare. Maile went back to where the housewife was still clutching the cell bars, now crying quietly. She had no hanky to offer, no way of drying tears. She occupied herself with taking apart her hairdo.

"Sorry you had to be in here when that happened. It's like that sometimes."

"Sounds like you're in here a lot."

"More often than necessary," Maile said.

"You're a prostitute?"

"Um, no. Suzie, that other girl that just left, thinks I am, and that I'm trying to move in on her turf."

The housewife looked Maile up and down. "You look pretty in that dress. Or you did a little while ago."

"Thanks. I'm afraid we all start to look like Suzie after a few hours in here. How long have you been in?"

"Since lunch."

"You haven't made bail?"

"Not till my husband finds me a lawyer. I don't know what's taking so long."

"You been in here before?" Maile asked.

The housewife shook her head.

"You drink a lot?"

"Not ever. Just got stupid this time."

Maile felt for the woman. She didn't seem to deserve to be locked in there with the others. But she'd been caught driving drunk, and that was enough. "What happened?"

"Had a fight with my husband. Getting really tired of those."

"Been there, done that."

"I told him I was going to the supermarket. I went to a bar instead. I only meant to have one drink, and then go home and tell him off, you know? But one drink led to another, and then a third. Before I knew it, I was out of money. I didn't know booze was so expensive."

"Yeah, my ex runs a bar. Big profits on that stuff, if someone runs the business right. I'm Maile, by the way."

"Celeste. What do you do?" the housewife asked.

"Tour guide."

"I bet you're good at it. How does a tour guide get thrown in jail?"

"Some stolen stuff showed up in my apartment with my fingerprints on it." Maile shrugged. "I don't have much of an alibi."

One by one, the hookers were released, while others were brought in. A middle-aged woman in business attire was led in, also smelling of booze. She took one step after the cell door slammed shut, twisted her ankle, and landed in a heap on the floor. When the woman started sobbing and complaining about her career being over, Maile left her to her straits on the floor.

"Is that what I look like?" Celeste asked after watching the businesswoman cry for a while.

"No."

"Thank goodness."

"Not yet, anyway."

Chapter Fourteen

When Maile's turn came to leave the cell, she was shown back to Detective Ota's desk where he was shuffling through papers waiting for her.

"What happened to you?" he asked when she sat down.

"Suzie Suzuki happened to me."

"Should've known. She's getting to be something of an embarrassment. Do you need to go to the hospital for that scratch on your cheek?"

Maile touched the spot. It was tender and warm. Of the thousands of scratches she'd had in her life, this one was worrisome. It came from the fingernail of a, well… "Is it that bad?"

"I have a first aid kit, if you like?"

"How impossible would it be to let me go to the bathroom?"

"Not impossible at all." He made a quick call, and five minutes later, a young front desk clerk in a simple police uniform arrived. Ota gave Maile a small kit from his desk drawer and told the clerk to take her to the public bathroom out front. "I want you to bring that kit back to me, Ms. Spencer."

"I will."

"I'm not done talking to you."

"Detective Ota, have I ever skipped out on you?"

"No, but someday you're going to turn dishonest on me, and I don't want it to be today. We have too many things to discuss."

When they got into the bathroom, the clerk stood acting like a guard as she watched Maile examine her cheek in the mirror. "Pretty dress."

"Thanks. It was nicer a few hours ago before a fight, a bus ride, riding in the back of a pickup truck across town, and getting soaked by the tears of a spurned bride."

"Sounds like a weird day."

"It was. Mind if I spend a few minutes washing off the last of this makeup?"

"I'm in no hurry. The station is quiet tonight."

"Night? What time is it?" Maile asked, splashing water on her face.

"Almost midnight."

"No wonder I'm so tired." She rubbed some alcohol wipes on the scratch to cleanse it. Finding some ointment, she swiped some of that on her cheek. After relieving herself after holding it all day, she adjusted the fit of her gown, shifting around inside of it. Since eating the spring rolls at lunch, hunger pangs had come and gone, and she wondered if she'd be able to talk the clerk into finding some food for her. Getting back to Ota's desk, she found a can of soda and a commercially made sandwich, something that would've come from a vending machine.

"Wouldn't it be easier to let me go home for a real meal?"

"You have real food at your place?" he asked, remaining busy with paperwork.

"No, but my mother does."

"Eat your sandwich before the expiration date passes."

It was cheese and a slice of something pink on white bread, with a smear of mustard. She inspected it closely. "I guess I should thank you for this, but I'm not feeling terribly grateful right now."

"I don't blame you."

"Okay, what do you want to badger me about?" she asked.

"I'm not going to…why do you always ask that?"

"Okay, interrogate ruthlessly."

He got his yellow pad again and slapped it down. He found a place he had bookmarked. "Okay, the first thing you need to know is that your old friend Prince Aziz is out of his federal holding cell."

"You mentioned that the other day." Maile choked down her mouthful of sandwich. "Where is he?"

"Not quite sure. Still on the island as far as anyone knows."

"Who let him out? That Mrs. Abrams from the federal district attorney's office?"

"It was her signature, but she got some sort of directive from higher up in Washington DC to let him out. And before you ask why, it was a matter of not having enough evidence to bring him to trial. She has you to thank for that."

"Yeah, me. It's my fault that a weirdo came all the way here from Khashraq to kidnap women to fill his harem."

"From what I've heard through the courthouse grapevine is that she has one month to find evidence to hold him over for a new trial or set him free."

"I know you have a lecture prepared for me, about how I just need to give up on worrying about him going to prison and let it go, blah blah, blah, but the idea of him propositioning women, and then drugging them to take home with him to be his weird slaves just makes me sick."

"Me, too. But Abrams has no evidence of that. All we have on him is solicitation. That's not worth the diplomatic…"

"I know. Not worth the diplomatic nightmare. He'd simply pay the fine, get on his private jet, and fly home."

"Mrs. Abrams wants me to talk to you about becoming involved as a witness in her case against him again."

Maile took a sip of her soda. "When I get an apology from her, and my nursing license is reinstated, then I'll think about it. Until then, forget it. She's getting nothing from me."

"Look, I don't want to be in the middle of game of female stubbornness. I already have enough of that in my life. What do you want me to tell her?"

"Tell Mrs. Abrams she can go…"

Ota put his hand up to stop her. "I can't say that to an officer of the federal courts."

"Tell her that if she provides her schedule for me well ahead of time, and respects my private life, and does something to help me get my nursing license reinstated, I'll be a witness in Aziz's trial." She watched as he wrote her demands down on his legal pad. "I don't want her yanking my chain like she did last time. Add that to the rest of my demands. May I go home now?"

"Not yet. But thank you for asking politely."

Maile sighed as loudly as she could when sitting back in the chair to sip her soda.

"I have someone tailing Aziz, just to make sure he doesn't stray too far."

"Who's that? Lefty Louie?"

"What kind of name is that?" he asked.

"You don't have Lenny the Snitch anymore. Why not some guy named Lefty Louie?"

"There's news about your husband," he said, shaking his head, and getting another legal pad.

"I'm not married. Free woman. No attachments to Robbie Smith or any other man, neither legal nor emotional."

"What about Turner?" Ota asked.

"What about him?"

"I thought you had something going on with him?"

"I thought so too, but apparently, Miss Wong from Chop Suey City has more to offer than I do."

Ota looked at the notes on his yellow pad. "Back to your husband…"

"Ex. What has he done to make me proud this time?"

"I'm arresting him."

"Cool. For?"

"Falsifying a legal business document."

"He really was cooking his books, or whatever it's called?"

"It's been discovered that he used falsified earnings data, and faked payment amounts for stock. Believe it or not, that's against the law."

That didn't make any sense to Maile. "But he just sold the place to his brother."

"Yes, to your boss at the tour company. Thomas is now proud owner of a cheap bar in Chinatown, along with the tour agency."

Maile crumpled her can and tossed it in the wastebasket. "And once again, I get nothing. I put all my spare earnings into that bar from my job as a nurse. Several years of hard work, down the drain."

"Sorry. I know how hard nurses work for their pay. What I need to know from you is if you knew anything about your ex's books being altered?"

"I was his sugar momma for keeping the place going. The dumbest thing I ever did was to not keep an eye on his books. I trusted him every step of the way." She sighed again. "That's not the only thing he was untrustworthy about."

"That's a definite no?" Ota asked.

"One hundred percent no."

"Just so you know, your boss is being investigated for collusion to commit a felony."

"Thomas had something to do with Robbie altering the books? That's doesn't make sense, but nothing does right now."

He finished writing something and put all his legal pads away. "Ready for a ride home?"

"I don't get to spend the rest of the night in the cell?"

"You can, if you like. I heard you were making a new friend in there."

"A lady named Celeste. I hope you guys went easy on her. It sounds like she made a really bad decision and got caught."

"I don't know. We're still waiting for her husband to send in a lawyer."

"What? She's still sitting in there?"

"We've called the husband a couple of times to see if he wants a public defender. He's not exactly Mister Responsibility."

"That's how Celeste made him out to sound. Do I get my phone back?"

He took it from his drawer and handed it over, along with her keys and the necklace. She was immediately on the phone, not to check for messages, but to make a call.

"Who're you calling?" Ota asked, standing. He had his car keys in one hand.

"A lawyer for Celeste."

"You know a lawyer that'll be interested in helping her at this time of night?"

"I know a great lawyer who owes me a favor." She hoped David Melendez wouldn't be too angry when he answered so late at night. "Hello, David? This is Maile Spencer."

"Hey, I was just talking to my cousin about you. In fact, she's right here. Hold on."

"Actually, I called to talk to you. I have a big favor to ask."

"After you helped Melanie so much with her daughter, anything. Name it."

"I'm at the police station right now…"

"Is everything okay? Are you in trouble?" he asked.

"It's not for me. I met someone here that's in a fix and isn't getting any help." She explained about Celeste sitting in a cell, waiting for her husband to bring a lawyer and bail her out.

"Sure. Melanie and I have been drinking coffee all evening talking about the good old days. I'm feeling a little wired right now, so I may as well do some work. What's her name?"

"Celeste Choi," Ota whispered.

Maile gave David the name. "I doubt they have much money to pay. Probably by morning they'll have a public defender anyway."

"Don't worry about it. Hold on. My cuz wants to talk to you."

Maile waited a moment until she heard a woman's voice take the phone from him. "Hello, Doctor...er, Mayor Kato?"

"It's easier if you call me Melanie. Everybody else does. You got away from the church before I could pay you for having Thérèse overnight. Can I bring you a check in the morning?"

Maile yawned when she checked the time. It was already two in the morning. "I'm supposed to take my mother to church in the morning and have a tour to give in the afternoon. Instead of paying me, just give the check to David. He's doing some work for me this morning. How's Thérèse? Did she say if she had a good time?"

"Thérèse spent the day talking about you naming her and a friend Keepers of the Kingdom? What was that about?"

Maile chuckled for the first time in hours. "Oh, some kahili were removed from a Hawaiian church and we went on something of a treasure hunt to find them. Just for fun. She and the other girl got along quite well."

"You certainly lead an interesting life. Having that other girl along made it even more fun. Now Thérèse wants to go to Ohio to visit Sammy."

"Does she have access to a computer and one of your credit cards?" Maile explained how Samantha paid for her flight by being sneaky.

"Thanks for the head's up. I'll make sure that doesn't happen."

Maile couldn't control her yawning and begged off the call.

"You need a meal?" Detective Ota asked while driving her home.

"I need a bed."

"Your place or your mother's?"

The bed was more comfortable at her mother's cottage, but she had privacy in her room. The last thing she wanted was to do a recap of the day's events with her mother, including what happened at the police station. She had at least a dozen messages from Lani, Lisa, and the other bridesmaids, all wanting her to call back as soon as possible. They would have to wait.

"I can go home to my personal crime scene?"

"You may. It was cleared during the evening by the CSI techs."

"Okay, fine. My place." She followed him through the station to the police parking garage. "What did Mrs. Taniguchi have to say to you?"

"She discovered I lied to her."

Maile was intrigued. "About?"

"That I really am the Ota boy she knows from the hongwanji."

Not so interesting right then. "What did she tell you about me? Did she turn on me? Do you guys still say that? Witnesses turning on each other?"

"Only the hardened criminals that're going to the big house."

"Seriously, what'd she say?"

"That you can do no wrong, firmly ensconced on a pedestal of righteousness."

"She should've seen me rolling around the floor of the cellblock, locked in a battle of hair pulling with Suzie."

"Despite that, she's quite fond of you."

"Then why does she give me such a hard time?" They stopped at the curb in front of her building. "Never mind. I don't care."

"Isn't that your worn duty, to care about others?" he asked.

"As nurse, daughter, sister, friend, or neighbor? Because I failed that as a wife."

"I doubt you've ever failed at anything."

Exhaustion had found every corner of Maile's body during the short ride home. "It's getting harder and harder to prioritize the things to care about these days."

"I do want to say one thing before letting you go," he said.

Even though there was little light in the dark car, she watched as the necklace sparkled in her hand. "Your usual warning not to interfere in your investigation?"

"Well, yes, that. But I just wanted to comment how nice you look in that dress. Quite elegant, regal."

It was something that her mother had said to Maile when she finished dressing that morning, that she looked very much like a queen from Hawaii's past. "Thanks. That means a lot to me."

"By the way, while you were busy fighting in the cellblock, I had someone take a look at that necklace. Those are real gems, and platinum. Your friends spent a pretty penny on that."

Maile looked at the sparkle one last time. "I guess I have to return it, since they didn't get married."

She tiptoed down the creaky wood hallway to her door. Along with her phone, Ota had returned her keys. That's where she had the necklace clasped, around the keychain. There were two notes thumbtacked to the door, one from Mrs. Taniguchi, and one from Rosamie. The one from her landlady stated only that she wanted to talk to Maile about something in the morning. The one from Rosamie started in her native language until that was scratched out and started over. It merely said that Rosamie had no choice about something, and that she was sorry.

"Whatever."

She went through the procedure of unlocking all the locks and pushed the door open. A security chain was across the gap, not allowing her access inside. She peeked through the gap. The kahili and quilt were gone, of course, but someone was on the bed, covered by a sheet. Maile was just about to run back down the stairs to see if Ota was still there when she recognized who it was in her bed.

"Oh, it's you. What're you doing here?"

Keepers of the Kingdom

Chapter Fifteen

The young man pulled the sheet up to cover his chest. "I didn't know where else to go."

"But you're in my bed."

"I came to talk to you and waited. I guess I got tired and fell asleep. Not many places to sit in here."

"You're in the bed, not on top of it." Maile pushed on the door again, straining against the security chain. She figured if she pushed hard enough, something would break loose. That would require finding a handyman to fix her door, something that was causing her new trouble right then. For as skinny as the young man was, there was very little risk of him hurting her. "Daniel, can you let me in, please? It's my apartment, not yours."

The male nurse that she used to work with at Honolulu Med, the one she got the kiss from the evening before, left the bed and opened the door for her. He gave her a smile that was somewhere between nervous and sad as she went past him into her room. She did a quick walk-through to see if everything was still there, not that she didn't trust him.

Hands on her hips, she stared him down. "Okay, why are you in my apartment?"

Daniel sat in the one chair that Maile had, something that went with her tiny kitchen table. "I needed to talk to someone. To you."

She had a pretty good idea of what it was about. Assuming he was going to be there for a while, she put the kettle on the stove for tea water. "How did you get in?"

"It wasn't easy. That old landlady found me knocking on your door and tried chasing me away."

"That must be what the note is about that I got from her."

"But I came back and knocked some more. Your neighbor across the hall peeked out and asked who I was."

"Rosamie?"

"I guess. I told her I needed to talk to you about something important. She finally let me in after I said we used to work together at the hospital."

"I'll have to talk to her about that." She poured two cups of hot water and put chamomile tea bags in each, giving him one. "Daniel, there are better times and places to talk about whatever's bothering you than this. You can't just barge into someone's home and expect to be welcomed."

"You did."

"And that might be changing pretty soon. In thirty minutes or less, what did you want to talk to me about? Because I have to get up in a few hours and take my mom to church."

"You know...about me, don't you?"

"I think so."

"You knew it when you kissed me?"

"That's what clinched it for me. In fact, I came to you for that kiss because I knew it would be safe. I knew you wouldn't read too much into it."

His hand-wringing went to his face, which also twisted into a knot. "Are you going to tell the others?"

"Pretty sure they already know your secret."

He hung his head. "Time to move again."

"Move? Why? Nobody cares." Maile knew she had some damage control to do with that comment. "What I mean is, nobody at work cares about how you identify. What they care about is how hard you work and that you take great care of your patients. That's what the people at the hospital care about. I don't know the rest of your friends to tell you about them."

"Don't have many."

She patted his hand and took their mugs to the sink to rinse. "That's another talk for another time. Right now, I need to go to bed."

Daniel made no moves toward the door.

"Daniel?"

"Can I stay the night?" he asked.

"Um…"

"Not for that. It just feels safe here."

"Not many places to sleep here, and that chair isn't very comfortable for more than a few minutes." She looked at his big puppy dog eyes and relented. "If you promise to stay on your side of the bed, you can stay. But if I feel one errant finger come anywhere near me, I'm breaking it off. And I don't mean your finger."

Maile figured it was best to sleep on top of the bed rather than under the sheet, and kept her gown on. She tumbled off to sleep with the idea that she was sleeping in a wedding gown with a gay man that was thinking of coming out of the closet.

***

As slender as Daniel was, he turned out to be a snorer. It was nearly loud enough to drown the alarm clock when it beeped. Maile left him behind when she went to the shower. Taking her gown off for the first time since early the previous morning, she was glad for the release from the taffeta and silk prison. A long shower got rid of the last of her makeup and goop in her hair, and twenty-four hours of body odor. Wrapped in two towels, she went to find Daniel already dressed. He handed her a mug of tea he'd made.

"Thanks," he said shyly.

"I didn't do anything." She tossed an outfit down on the bed that he'd already made. "You mind turning around? I need to dress."

"I'm not sure what to do now."

"Find a professional to talk to about all the stuff you're going through. I don't mind lending an ear from time to time, but I haven't gone through any of what you're going through. I'd only make a mess out of it."

"No, I mean today."

She pulled a blouse over her head. "You have the weekend off?"

"I work this evening."

"Oh, yeah, those split weekend schedules. I hated those." She wrapped her skirt around her waist and buttoned it closed. "Come to church with my mom and brother."

"Church?"

"The congregation isn't big and we're rather informal."

"You go to a Hawaiian church, though."

She stroked a brush through her hair a few times. "Everybody's welcome."

"Even people trying to figure out things in their life?"

"Especially them. That's the point of going to church."

While Maile locked her door as they left, Rosamie peeked from her doorway. She looked Daniel up and down. "Going to breakfast?"

Maile had no time for sharing gossip, or for explanations that morning. She dragged Daniel down the hall with her, fleeing her neighbor. "Church, and in a hurry."

The gauntlet wasn't done, though. At the bottom of the stairs, Mrs. Taniguchi waited with crossed arms.

Maile doubled the speed of their exit. "Yes, I know, Mrs. Taniguchi. No men in the rooms after dark."

Her brother Kenny was already waiting at the curb in a borrowed car when they got to the sidewalk. Kealoha was in the back seat, her usual spot. Maile pushed Daniel into the front seat and got in the back with her mother. Kenny nodded at Daniel before getting into the light Sunday morning traffic.

"Who's that?" her mother asked in Hawaiian. "New hoa kane?"

"Not my boyfriend."

"Just came from your place first thing in the morning. What's that called?"

"It's called a friend and old co-worker having some trouble. And his name is Kaniela. Daniel."

"You solved his trouble the old-fashioned way?"

"Mom! No, we just talked about stuff."

"What kind of stuff?" her mother asked. "Because late at night, only one kind of stuff a man and woman talk about."

"He's mahu, okay? No one else knows, so don't bring it up."

Kealoha looked through her purse for something. "Mahu very important people to the Hawaiians."

"I know, but there're still some people in the world who shun them."

Kealoha leaned forward and tapped Daniel on the shoulder. "Kaniela, this is for you. Keep it with you when troubles come haunting."

"Mom, he doesn't speak Hawaiian." She saw the small thing in her mother's hand, what she was trying to give Daniel. She couldn't believe her mother was handing it over so easily to someone she didn't know. She also knew not to argue about it. "Daniel, my mother wants to give you something."

He took the small amulet in his hand. It was a tiny tiki, carved from koa wood that had turned dark over time, attached to a frayed leather lanyard. For all of her life, Maile had seen that somewhere near her mother, but had never asked many questions about it. For as religious and active at church as they were, Maile and her mother both felt deeply about the religion of their Hawaiian roots.

"You're giving him that?" Kenny asked.

"Keneka, hush. Not about you," Kealoha said.

"What is it?" Daniel asked.

Maile explained. "It's a small tiki in the form of Kuka'ilimoku, one of the primary gods from ancient Hawaii."

"Oh, thanks."

"Ku main god back then," Kealoha said, speaking as if 'back then' happened only a few years ago. "Akua of war, politics, so many things."

Daniel looked back at Maile for an explanation.

"Kuka'ilimoku was also considered dualistic, the god of dualism, of opposites."

Daniel gave it a closer scrutiny. "Oh."

"My mother and I believe it will bring you some solace when you're feeling the most troubled."

"But I'm not Hawaiian."

"Like I said earlier, everyone's welcome, Daniel."

"You keep that near you all the time," Kealoha said, tapping him on the shoulder again. "Very private. Not for sharing with others. When you're done with troubles, bring back to me, no one else."

When they got to church, Maile introduced Daniel to others, even when he acted shy around them, acting like a pea out of its usual pod. When she spotted someone she hadn't seen there in ages, she took Daniel over for an introduction.

"Daniel, this Marg...Mark. He's an old friend. He might be feeling a little uncomfortable being here today, also."

Daniel and Mark shook hands. Dressed in a loose-fitting suit and necktie, he was actually Margaret, the kahili expert at the museum Maile went to a couple of days before. Maile watched their eyes, and maybe she was reading something into their expressions, but they both seemed to relax as they talked. If they recognized something in each other, it was fine with her. The two of them were on life-changing trajectories right then, going in tangential directions, but maybe they could find something in common to lean on.

Or maybe she was making a mess of things. She wasn't sure about anything anymore.

The church had no piano or organ, but a guitar player came occasionally to play music. When he began to strum, the small congregation took their seats in pews. Maile led her mother and brother to their usual pew they'd occupied since when her mother was a child. Daniel followed them closely. Before sitting, Kealoha reached to take his hand.

"Sit with me."

When Daniel complied, Maile took her usual position at her mother's other side, with Kenny next to her. As usual, Kenny took his Bible from its place next to the hymnal, flipped through it for a moment, and put it back. Maile looked over at what her mother was doing. She held Daniel's hand in hers, and was muttering quiet prayers. Daniel wasn't nearly as distressed as Maile thought he might be.

***

At the end of the service, the congregation milled around in the sunshine outside. Mark talked to a few people who had figured out who he was. Maile worried for a moment about acceptance, and that Mark was there that day because she'd invited him to return. When she saw hand shaking between old friends rather than scorn, she was able to relax a little. She still had Daniel to fret over, though.

"I like your mom," Daniel said to Maile after taking her aside.

"Thanks. I'll tell her that."

"There's something special about her. I don't know what it is."

Maile was glad he felt it. Not everyone did. "I'm glad you feel that way. Are you going to be okay?"

"I'll be fine. Sorry about all the drama last night."

"You're allowed a moment of drama every now and then. We all are."

"What's the deal with Mark?" he asked, looking past her for a moment.

Maile looked to see Mark still chatting with others.

"Used to come here all the time until a few years ago. There's something about him you might need to know."

"I think I already do."

"Well, my mom looks ready to go," Maile said, trying to lead him to the parking lot.

"Mark's giving me a ride home. We might hang out for a while."

"Oh." For some reason, Maile kissed him on the cheek, then quickly wiped off the small smudge of lipstick.

Kenny took Maile to the Manoa Tours office next to meet her driver Lopaka there.

"Yesterday, bridesmaid," her mother said. "Today tour girl."

"Guide, Mom. And let's hope today goes better than yesterday."

"Really have to work on a Sunday?"

"Need to take these tours when they come along. I'm not sure how much longer Thomas will be in business."

"Why?" Kenny asked.

"It seems the Smith brothers aren't entirely honest in their business dealings, even with each other. Anyway, even if he gets shut down by the city, I might start a new job pretty soon."

"Finally getting your nurse license back?" her mother asked.

"I might be getting some help from Mrs. Abrams in setting up a new licensing board hearing."

"She caused you too much trouble already. You'd be back to work already if it wasn't for her."

"I'm being careful."

"Go back to work at the same place?" her mother asked.

"I've been thinking of trying something else. Still in nursing, but a little different."

"Another one of your big secrets? Keeping so many secrets from me lately."

"Not a secret. I'm still trying to decide. You'll be the first to know when I do."

Kealoha gave Maile's hand a squeeze. "Whatever it is, you'll be expert in no time."

Maile chuckled. "Or the biggest flop ever."

"Where you go guiding today?" her mother asked, just as Kenny got them to the Manoa Tour office.

"Lyon Arboretum."

"Nice there. Going to the falls?"

"Of course. That's the highlight of every tour to the arboretum."

Her mother took the *ilima* flower lei off from around her neck and gave it to Maile. "Put on."

Maile did as she was told. "For why?"

"Take on hike, make offer when no one watching."

Maile knew exactly what her mother meant and made the tentative plan for the lei. The bright yellow *ilima* was the flower of Oahu, and one of the flowers that represented Hawaiian royalty.

Lopaka was just finishing with drying the windows of the van. "Eh, brah. Ready to show off our hometown to the tourists?"

"Howzit, Maile. Some deal yesterday."

"You're telling me."

"Talk to Lani since?" he asked.

"A little afraid to. She took her mother on her honeymoon. Hopefully, she's having some fun and not spending all her time sticking pins in a doll of Ronald."

"That guy deserve it, if you ask me." He looked her up and down for a moment. "Going for hike up to the falls dressed like that?"

"Just came from church. Should be okay. Not gonna rain."

"How you know? Rain all the time in the Manoa Valley. You know that."

"I'm not gonna let it rain," Maile said, climbing aboard the tour bus.

Lopaka got the bus going through traffic toward Waikiki hotels. "I suppose you have some sort of direct line to Lono?"

"God of rainfall? I'm hoping I do today."

"Also god of fertility. You got something going I don't know about?"

She giggled at the thought of spending the night in bed with Daniel. Maybe the most interesting thing about it was that nothing happened between them. "Nothing worth telling Lono about."

Her group that day included men and women with a rugged edge to them, and dressed in expensive outdoor clothes. They introduced themselves as being from New Zealand, adding they were on a yearly junket to somewhere in the world that offered unusual plants. That was something Maile had been studying in the months since becoming a tour guide, adding names of plants, trees, and birds to her tours, along with ancient legends.

"Well, you've come to the right place. The arboretum is home to several hundred types of plants and trees, many of which we'll see close-up on the trail to the falls."

"That's what we're looking forward to the most," Oliver said. He seemed like the leader of the small group. He also had the most expensive camera hanging from around his neck. "The upper part of the valley."

Maile gave her usual tour lecture about the Manoa Valley, one of the rainiest places on the leeward side of the Island of Oahu. She watched for the small heritage center that was a yearly field trip site while in grade school, and then the school itself. Not far from there was her mother's cottage, and the Chinese cemetery that was a popular tourist destination, more for the possibility of capturing a ghostly sighting than for the graves. It wasn't much further beyond where the road began to wind up into the steeper part of the valley, leaving houses and the city behind. It was another world here, with trees creating canopies that shaded the forest floor below.

There were many legends about what the forest kept hidden, not all of them cheerful. Maile had visited those lower slopes of the Ko'olau Range many times, but had never spent the night—for good reason. Some of the stories she'd heard were a little too believable to be dismissed easily. Every cultural group on the island had their own creepy tales to tell: the Japanese spoke quietly of *kappa* water spirits that live in the pool at the base of the falls; the Chinese feared the restless spirits that roamed from the cemetery; haoles always complained of getting chicken skin for no reason at all; and the Hawaiians knew the place to be sacred, not to be messed with at the risk of sacrilege. If all that wasn't enough, a tropical bacteria lived in the water at the base of the falls, something that could cause serious illness if someone drank or swam in it too much. Not to mention the occasional rockfall from the cliff face. As beautiful as the forest and falls were, Maile knew better than to spend too much time there.

She needed to focus on what she was talking about to get her mind, and stomach, off the curves in the road. Lopaka must've noticed something was going on with her and pulled over into a turnout.

"What's wrong?" she asked, feeling more blood drain from her face as her stomach continued to do tricks.

"Your color's not so good."

"Might've eaten something wrong for breakfast."

"You ate?"

"Not much, but it isn't sitting right." When Lopaka opened the door for fresh air, Maile noticed a rainbow. Looking out the door, she saw it spanned from one side of the valley to the other, the way they often do there. "I told you Lono would show up today."

"Maybe you can ask Lono to cure what's ailing you right now."

Maile ate a couple of antacid tablets and washed them down with water. "All I need is a good night of sleep."

Her group wasn't particularly excited about seeing the rainbow, so after a few deep breaths of fresh air, they got started driving again. She still needed to keep busy chatting, though. She turned on her headset and started her sales pitch of her home island.

"The banyan trees on this island are known to house spirits. There's one at Iolani Palace that you may have seen on your tour there yesterday. There's another at that Chinese cemetery we passed a few minutes ago that's said to be haunted. And we'll find another at the beginning of the trail to the falls."

"We read about Night Marchers in this valley," Charlotte said. She was the tallest and seemed paired with Oliver, maybe the shortest in the group. While she for some odd reason reminded Maile of Big Bird, Oliver reminded her of Elmo, with his bright red hair, easy smile, and large nose. While the others in the group introduced themselves as botanists and wildlife photographers, Charlotte had said she was a police officer back in Auckland. Big Bird turned out to be a cop with a funny accent.

"Yes, that's right. They come down the cliff and through the valley on certain nights of the month. In fact, one legend states they pass through a pair of banyans along the trail."

"Why those two banyans?" someone asked from the back of the bus.

"Those two trees have grown up closely intertwining with each other and now seem as one.

Somehow, nature has allowed a gap to remain between them, which the trail we're taking today goes through. It's also where the Night Marchers pass."

"Almost sounds like sacred ground," Charlotte said.

"Many of the valleys on the island are."

"Who exactly are the Night Marchers?" someone else asked. Two men sat together that Maile had already secretly named Bert and Ernie.

"In ancient times, the ali'i, or royalty, on each island had to defend their island from other ali'i and their warriors. Bloody battles were waged, often until few warriors remained alive. Most of the time, very little was resolved, until Kamehameha the Great was able to unite all the islands under one rule. That's when the true Hawaiian monarchy started." During one long, sweeping curve, her stomach flipped, and then flopped, churning her meager breakfast. Running up the long road late at night was no problem, but having a set of wheels beneath her was what caused the trouble every trip through the narrow valley. "Anyway, it's those long-dead that march down the valley on certain nights of the month."

"Not during the full moon, is it?" Charlotte asked.

"That's exactly when. The night before, the night of, and the night after the fullest phase of the moon. Why?"

"Tonight's the full moon," Oliver said.

"Oh. Well, we're here during the day time, and the Marchers appear at night." She decided to toss in, just for fun, "Usually."

"I read that if we see Night Marchers coming our way, we're supposed to hide?" Bert asked.

"That's right. You lie down on your side and face away, playing dead. They should ignore you, but if you make eye contact with even just one of them, they'll stab you with a spear and take your soul with them, forcing you to march with them forever more."

"Tough crowd," Charlotte said.

Maile saw a straight stretch of road; a reprieve from the gastric upheaval was coming. "Best not to mess with our island spirits."

They made a potty stop at a visitor's center and visited a small gazebo and fishpond before starting on their hike. A wedding would be starting there, with everyone dressed in aloha attire. A young Japanese woman was marrying a haole, and his side of the family was under-represented with only his parents there. Maile's group left them alone when the minister decided to start the wedding ceremony.

With one last glance at the woman getting married, Maile couldn't help but think they knew each other.

"Okay, let's gear up," Oliver announced to his group. With that, they removed their sneakers and laced on sturdy hiking boots. After that, they each put on knapsacks or fanny packs, loaded with high-energy snacks, water bottles, first aid kits, and camera gear. Lopaka watched closely, and to Maile it looked like they were preparing for an ascent on Kilimanjaro.

"You know it's only a mile and a half altogether, from here to the falls and back again?"

"We're always prepared," he said.

She dug through her bag for a bottle of sun screen/bug repellant lotion. After putting a heavy layer on her face and arms, she offered it to her guests.

"Dealt with mosquitoes before," Oliver said. "You should see what they have in Borneo. Mozzies are the national bird there."

"Suit yourself." To finish preparing, Maile put her phone in one pocket of her loose skirt, and a small folded plastic rain poncho in the other. Keeping a bottle of water in her hand, she kicked off her flat shoes and left them in the bus. After that, she handed out more of the plastic ponchos to her group, each with the Manoa Tours logo stenciled on it. Folded the way they were, they weren't any bigger than a pocket packet of tissues. Most of them were stuffed in knapsack pockets.

"Where are your boots?" Charlotte asked.

"Generally don't need them. The trail is easy to negotiate, and often muddy. Easier just to rinse my feet when we get back to the van."

"What about the soles of your feet?" Oliver asked.

"I'm trying to toughen them up for a marathon in a couple of weeks." Maile raised a foot to show them the sole of it. "Spend more time barefoot than wearing shoes, including on this trail. I'll be okay."

Oliver didn't look convinced as he led his troops off into the forest.

Chapter Sixteen

When they got to the pair of banyans she had told them about, the group crowded together beneath them and posed for pictures. Lopaka and Maile snapped pictures of them with expensive cameras. Maile felt some misgivings about what was taking place, or maybe it was her stomach still turning over from the drive there.

"Maile, joined us!" called Charlotte.

"You know what?" She snapped one last picture of the group, hoping she had the camera aimed properly. "I'm just a little too superstitious to mess around with legends. I don't mind talking about them, but I draw the line at being a part of them."

As they walked along the dirt trail packed hard by the thousands of other feet that followed it each year, Maile pointed out some of the more prominent trees in the forest.

"It's okay, Maile," Charlotte said. "They're all botanists. They know all about these trees. What we'd like to hear about are the legends of Oahu. Tales like that of the Night Marchers you told us about earlier."

"There's an unusual legend about something that took place here in the Manoa Valley. Sort of a love story, so I don't know how true it is."

"Not a hopeless romantic?" Charlotte asked.

"Not after what happened yesterday. I'll tell you about that later. But many years ago, the wind and rain gave birth to a child who grew into a great beauty. When she was old enough to marry, Kahalaopuna was captured by Kauhi, one of the shark gods. When she spurned him, he got so angry that he killed her and hid her body somewhere in this forest."

"Around here?" Bert or Ernie asked. Even though she had nicknamed them, Maile was getting them confused. They had drawn close to listen to the story.

"Could've been anywhere in here," Maile said. "Legend has it a koa tree grew over her grave."

"Seems like a good place to hide a body," Charlotte muttered.

"For the longest time, Kahalaopuna's spirit wandered the forest, moaning throughout the night. People who heard her complaining moans said it was always on the same night of the month as her murder, the night of the new moon when the night was darkest."

"Giving me chills, Maile," Charlotte said, rubbing the chicken skin on her arms.

"Eventually, her withered, half-rotten body was found by Mahana, one of the ali'i chiefs of the valley. He took her bones back to the village where the kahuna brought life back into her, and united her soul and body again."

"Wow, pretty powerful medicine man."

"Actually, that kahuna was a woman. The most powerful usually are."

"That's the end of the story?" Charlotte asked. "Where's the romance?"

"Once Kahalaopuna was brought back, she fell in love with Mahana, her rescuer. But before she gave herself to him, she wanted her revenge. So Mahana went off in search of Kauhi, and baked him alive in an imu, an underground cooking pit."

"Like they use at luaus?"

"Just like that."

"What a way to go," said Charlotte, rubbing her arms again.

"Once that was done, Kahalaopuna and Mahana were given the valley to use for the rest of their lives." Maile spotted a group that was coming down the trail toward them and wondered why so many were grouped together. It looked as though they were carrying something between them, and hoped it wasn't hunters bringing a dead pig down from the mountains in front of her group. "To finish the story, every month, on the darkest night, that of the new moon, some people can still hear Kahalaopuna screaming for help in the forest. That's why authorities don't want people taking the trails after sunset. I don't know if it's true, though."

When the approaching group neared them, Maile saw they were well-organized and all wearing the same uniforms, that of rescue paramedics. When they passed by, the ones in the lead were carrying a simple litter, with a fully-clothed man on it. He was awake and looking around, but in obvious pain.

"What happened?" she asked the man at the rear of the parade.

"He was rock climbing, showing off by trying to go up the waterfall. He discovered water always wins every contest."

"He's okay?"

"Broken leg. Lucky it wasn't his head."

They were almost to the waterfall, the playful sound of it coming through the woods. More people were leaving, and from the sounds of it, they were following after the man with the broken leg. Most of her group had gone ahead, while Maile struggled to keep going. It was Lopaka who came to her aid in getting over a large log.

"You really don't feel well, do you?"

"I've felt better. I wish I could go back to the van and wait for them, but I doubt I'd make it."

"Not hapai?"

"Oh, shut up." She finished her bottle of water while panting through a heavy sweat. "Why does everybody ask me that when I don't feel well?"

"You should be in better shape than this. Running that big race in a couple weeks. Still running all the time, right?"

"Every chance I get. Never felt stronger. I don't know why I feel like this today."

"Too much bad news yesterday finally catching up with you."

"I don't know. It's almost like I'm being warned away from the falls."

"You and your legends. What do you want me to do?" he asked.

"Just help me over this log. If I can splash some water on my face at the pond, I'll perk up."

He helped her clear the massive koa log, but it was slippery from rain and time, and she slipped off the other side of it, slamming her big toe into a rock.

"Never heard you use those words before," he said, helping her up again.

"Stick around." She began limping down the trail toward the pond. "I know more."

"That guy's gonna give you all kinds of grief for not wearing shoes."

"Tickle Me Elmo? Let him. His boots cost more than what you and I make in a week."

Just as they got to where waterfall mist wafted through the air, there was a child's shriek. A woman screamed right after.

"Now what?" Maile complained.

"Sounded like a kid. Not our problem," Lopaka said.

When they got to the pool at the base of the waterfall, there was a small group huddled around a boy and a woman. The woman was in a slow-motion freak-out the way a mother would be with a hurt child. Oliver and Charlotte were busy offering their opinions on what should be done. A uniformed pair leftover from the earlier rescue was still there, packing up their supplies. Only wanting to soak her stubbed toe in the cool water, Maile limped over to the boy to take a look.

The boy's mother was struggling with something as her son continued to wail. That's when she noticed the welt on his thigh.

"What happened?" she asked.

"Timmy was stung by a bee."

Maile noticed the thing in her hands was an Epipen, something used to prevent anaphylaxis. "He's allergic to bee stings?"

"We just figured it out a while back. I've never had to use one of these before. But that sting is getting big fast." She held the device in the air. "Anybody know how it works?"

Maile took it from her, prepared the two ends, held it in her fist, and pressed it on the boy's thigh. "This might hurt."

"Okay."

After the self-activating device did its work, she handed it back to the mother.

"How long does it take to work?" the mother asked.

"Should be right away." Using one of the fake nails leftover from the day before, Maile was able to flick away the stinger that was still lodged in the boy's skin. She noticed that the two last rescuers were still there, watching. "It looks like you're going to be okay. But you know what? I bet these two nice rescue guys would be glad to hike back down the trail with you so your mom can take to the hospital."

"We sure will! What about it, sport? Think you can walk all the way back to the car?"

He nodded as he got his feet under him. His mother put her arm around his shoulders as they left the falls. Once they were gone, the others went off in search of what else waited to be discovered. Lopaka sat next to Maile on the rock she occupied.

"Saved another one, Mai."

"Used an Epipen. No biggie."

"It was to that kid and his mother."

Having broken into a heavy sweat, she waved her hat at her face. "I wish it was so easy to get rid of this car sickness. Never lasts this long."

He handed her his bottle of water to sip. "Why don't you soak your toe in the water?"

"Ugh. I can't move from here or I might turn into a gastric volcano."

"What's with the lei? You don't usually wear one on tours."

Even though it had been over her shoulders for the last two hours, she'd forgotten about the lei from her mother.

"I forgot all about this. I'm supposed leave it here with a prayer when no one is looking."

"How do you keep all your religious practices straight?"

She tried taking a cooling breath, but the heat felt stifling. "I don't."

"I can keep the others occupied for a couple minutes while you do your thing with the lei."

Maile limped a few feet over to the edge of the pond. The knot in her hair had come loose on the hike and she bundled it together again, using her silk scarf to hold it tight. Sun filtered through the trees, warming her shoulders. A pair of birds flew over the water chasing each other in a game only they understood. She wished she could fly away to a new place, leaving today behind.

On other visits, there had always been waders in the water, usually only knee-deep. This time, maybe because of the fallen climber rescue earlier, or maybe because of the signs warning of the bacteria disease in the water, visitors were staying clear. That gave Maile the chance to toss the lei into the water where it floated on the surface while water fell from above. She set her empty hands on her thighs, palms aimed at the heavens, and recited a quiet prayer. Once the task was done, she eased her feet into the water and let the churning bubbles scrub the blood from her big toe. It wasn't long before her troubled stomach settled while watching the lei swirl through the splashing pond. When it finally sank, she took a deep breath and looked up toward the top of the falls. Near the top was a faint rainbow in the mist.

"Thanks, Lono."

Lopaka came back to her a few minutes later. "Doing okay?"

"Fine." She lifted her feet from the water, showing off her clean toe. "All fixed up. Just needed to say a prayer."

Lopaka chuckled. "To who?"

"Same as always. Anyone that was listening."

"Most days, I think they're all listening to you, Mai."

There was a foreign-accented voice of a woman speaking English as she approached the pond from the trail. Maile knew Chinese tourists tended to batch together in large groups and took over sites on their arrival, with a tour leader waving a flag around, often talking into a bullhorn. Wanting to avoid that, Maile decided it was time to gather her group and leave.

But it was the next voice she heard that kept her rear end locked to the rock she was perched on.

"It's beautiful here, one of my favorite places to visit on the island," the man said.

Maile felt Lopaka's hand on her shoulder, giving her a comforting squeeze. "Maybe we should go."

"You know, I like sitting here." Maile glanced over at her group, who were still lounging and snacking. "They're not ready to go and we still have an hour to go on this tour. What's the hurry?"

"Come on, Mai. You don't want to do this in front of tour guests."

Maile continued to listen to the couple chat as they got to the edge of the pool. To hide, she put her hat back on and tugged it low over her face. "Do what?"

"Confront her."

"Not gonna confront her. It's the jerk with her that needs a fingernail in the eye."

"I see trouble coming," Lopaka said, wandering off.

From under the wide brim of her hat, she took up the task of watching the couple, obviously on a date, soak their feet in the water just as Maile was. There was some chitchat, followed by playful flirting. She couldn't see everything that happened, but there was a moment when their faces were close together. Too close.

After that, the girl slipped out of her shorts and top, revealing a one-piece swimsuit beneath. Wading into the shallow water, she giggled while scooping and splashing some back at her date.

"Oh, brother," Maile whispered, tugging the brim of her hat even lower.

The man stayed on the rock, watching and talking to his friend play in the water. She was the only one in the pool, enjoying herself immensely. Other visitors noticed and watched them, and a few packed up their things and left. After a few more minutes, Oliver and Charlotte came over to Maile.

"Time to leave, isn't it, Maile?"

Maile finally broke her gaze on the couple and snapped out of her contemplations. She checked the time. "I suppose so."

Getting up, she made one last glance at the couple. Now the man was looking back at her. After saying something to his date, he came over to Maile as her group packed their things in knapsacks.

"Enjoying the falls, Officer Turner?"

"Hi, Maile. Nice day, isn't it?"

"The weather? Couldn't be better. Is that Miss Chop Suey from Wong's Restaurant?"

"I think you got it mixed up."

"No, I didn't. And my name is Ms. Spencer. Please remember that."

"Doing tours on Sundays now?" Brock asked.

"Have been for quite a while. Need to earn a living." She took her hat off to wave air into her face. "Didn't you see the signs? The water looks clean, but there's bacteria in it. Miss Chop Suey could get sick."

"Don't call her that."

"Whatever." She started making her way over the rocks surrounding the pool. "I don't care about either one of you."

Waving her hat to cool her face, she led her group through the forest, the soles of her feet barely feeling the ground as she went.

Chapter Seventeen

As they hiked, Charlotte joined Maile at her side.

"Had a few words with that guy. Who is he?"

"Nobody…anymore."

Charlotte's long legs matched Maile's rapid stride. "Old boyfriend?"

"Almost a boyfriend. Almost dated, anyway."

"Pretty girl he was with. Tough competition."

"Too bad for me." Thinking of Brock dating the waitress from the restaurant, and how she'd never go back to it, made Maile think of police work. "You said you're a police officer back in Auckland, right?"

"Not a patrol officer. I work in investigations of crimes, sort of behind the scenes work."

"You might be the right person to talk to."

"About?" Charlotte asked.

"Something happened here a few days ago. A pair of flags were stolen from a public building that many people have access to."

"Oh, a mystery to solve!"

"The police seemed to be stumped about it. But the next day, the flags were found in the possession of a private citizen, in her home, along with something else that had been stolen from another location. The woman claims she knows nothing about them or how they got into her apartment, but when the police checked for fingerprints, the only ones they found were hers, plus a few smudged ones that couldn't be identified. The woman is now a suspect, of course."

"Naturally, and she should be," Charlotte said.

"She continues to deny knowing anything about how the flags got in her home, or why her prints are on the poles. Is it possible the police have made a mistake?"

"You're wondering if the police are somehow planting her prints on the flag poles to make her look guilty?"

"Not really that. More like they got data mixed up in the system?"

Charlotte shook her head. "Probably not, unless the detective and the crime scene technicians are thoroughly incompetent. There might be a situation in which the suspect has the exact same name as someone else already in the system, and if there was another crime that involved flags. But even so, they'd get that figured out after a while."

"The suspect has an unusual name. Why would her prints be showing up and not someone else's?" Maile asked.

"I can't answer that without knowing more of the details of the case. I bet since the flags were recovered so easily, and not a big ticket item with high monetary value, the police might not be putting as much effort into finding the culprit as in other cases. I'm sure they have bigger crimes to solve."

"The thing about the flags is that they're historically important," Maile explained. "Sort of like Martha Washington sewed them herself."

"Oh yes, the Star Spangled Banner," Charlotte said. "Still, someone would need to show evidence of their historical significance and monetary value to classify it as a serious crime that would take precedence over violent crimes that need to be investigated."

"I suppose. But it's the fingerprints that keep coming back to my mind. I keep wondering who might've put those flags in the woman's apartment."

"For more complex cases involving fingerprints, in Auckland we use something called Egyptian blue as a dusting powder after we've already collected prints with regular powder."

"I've never heard of that."

"Very unusual stuff. Egyptian blue is a type of calcium copper chemical that was used in ancient Egypt as a blue tint for paint. They used it to decorate mummies and tomb walls, and on papyrus. It's a very pretty color. But centuries later, the way they made it was lost, at least until modernday scientists were able to recreate it."

"Why is it so special to the police?" Maile asked.

"The special thing about it is that it can be crushed and ground into very fine powder before being applied, finer than the usual dust we use to collect fingerprints. The really great thing about it is how it glows under certain lighting conditions."

"You mean it's fluorescent?"

"I think the word is luminescent. Since the powder is so fine, it can stick to very light prints that coarser powders can't. When the right type of light is shone on the surface that has been dusted with Egyptian blue, we can find latent prints that were otherwise invisible. Its use is changing police investigation work as much as DNA is."

"So, if the Honolulu police use this blue powder on the flag poles, they might find other prints besides mi…the suspect's?"

"Right. But it's very expensive and not easy to come by. Not many departments are using it. Honestly, we're only trialing it in Auckland and I'm not sure we'll keep using it, simply because of the expense."

"How do I get some of this stuff? I mean…"

"I think your secret is out, Maile. As far as I know, the kind that is used by police departments is only available to them. If you know the investigating detective, you might be able to make a request for blue to be used in the investigation."

"I get the idea that they're on a tight budget. They also don't like it when I…someone interferes with their work."

"Might be time to get a lawyer to help you. Maybe their influence will accomplish something?"

Maile knew the exact person to talk to. She'd been getting a lot of favors from him lately, though. "Maybe."

They were back to the van by then, and while the others changed from their boots, she rinsed her feet at a spigot behind the visitor center. By then, she had dirt and mud up to her knees, and smudges on her dress. So much for dressing in pretty clothes to boost her mood. After seeing Officer Turner and Miss Wong at the waterfall, finding a good mood seemed impossible.

When she finally got home, she got her door open as quietly as possible, hoping not to attract the attention of Rosamie. From the savory scent lingering in the hallway, it was dinnertime across the hall, and as hungry as she was right then, she just needed—craved—the peace and quiet that only solitude could bring.

After a long shower, Maile sat cross-legged on her bed, searching the pictures in her phone. She knew there were two in there that needed to be deleted. One was of her and Officer Turner dressed in eveningwear for a garden party they went to a few weeks before, to work a simple undercover job for the police. After looking at it for a moment, something she'd looked at a hundred times before with big plans in her mind and great hopes in her heart, she hit delete. Scrolling for a few more minutes, she found the other image, taken by another police officer of her and Turner seated at the table next to each other at Chop Suey City. That one was a lot easier to delete, since Miss Wong's hip was in the background. Her task complete, she tossed the phone aside and flopped onto her back.

"I should eat." Still wrapped in towels, she inspected her refrigerator. There was a note on the outside from Rosamie, that she had put a 'surprise' inside. There was more to the note, but she yanked the door open to see what had been left for her. Even a tub of leftovers would fill the void that had been growing all day. "Well, at least there's something for dinner."

Inside were the few things she'd left there, bottles of condiments, a jar of pickles, half-eaten cup of yogurt, one mini-doughnut, and a rubbery carrot. All that had been pushed aside to make space for a large pastry box. Another note was taped to the top of that.

All my gals get some, and you get the top layer. Thanks for being there for me on my "special" day, Mai! Enjoy! (You might want to keep the B & G from the top for your own cake. Wedding bells might be ringing soon!)

It was signed by Lani, with a large red heart at the end.

"B and G? Oh, Bride and Groom."

She took the box out and set it on the counter. Opening the lid, she found the top layer of Lani's wedding cake inside, complete with the typical plastic bride and groom holding hands. They had been hand painted, with tiny cheerful smiles and large hopeful eyes.

"Where'd this come from? Lani's on her vacay with her mom."

She looked at Rosamie's note for an explanation.

Your friend Lisa came by and asked to put something in your fridge. Lani didn't want to see it again, whatever that means.

Taking the bride and groom from the top, she tossed that into the kitchen waste can.

"Wedding bells my…" She stopped to scold herself. "Been swearing too much lately."

Maile lopped off a big chunk of cake and took it back to the bed. Sitting cross-legged again, she ate the cake with her fingers. She put in an ear bud and looked for music on her phone, but all she found were love songs, something she didn't want to hear right then. Next, she looked for online sources of the Egyptian blue powder Charlotte had told her about. What little information there was about it was limited to law enforcement officials and laboratory scientists. Finishing the cake as quickly as she could, she picked frosting from under her acrylic nails.

Going back to the kitchen to wash her hands, she tossed the remaining cake in the trash. She stared at it at the bottom of the trash bin for the longest time. Swirls of decorations were crushed, and frosting was peeling loose from the cake. The plastic bride and groom had been splattered by an explosion of icing, their oddly-painted smiles almost mocking her.

"That's the way it goes sometimes."

She slammed the lid back down on the trash bin. After settling on her bed again, she checked the time.

"Eight-thirty in the evening. That's late enough to go to bed."

She turned off the lamp and pulled the sheet over her. In the dark, she stared at the water stain on the ceiling.

"Late enough if I'm a hundred years old." She turned the light on again. Grabbing her phone, Maile started scrolling again. It wasn't to look for a date, but for help. "Surely David Melendez will know how to find some of that Egyptian blue stuff."

Before she could dial the number, her phone rang with a call. It was from Melanie Kato, Thérèse's mother.

"I was looking for an address to send you a check for all the extra time you spent taking care of my daughter. All I can find is a place called the Manoa House. Is that where you live?" Melanie asked.

"She mostly took care of herself. The Manoa House is more of a community center and private library that people of Hawaiian heritage use to meet. I think she's ready to move in there, but she'd have visitors dropping in every day."

"I think my daughter mentioned it once or twice. Where should I send the check?"

"You know what? I was just thinking about asking your cousin David for some help with something. I asked him for another big favor for a friend, but now I have something new to work on. The thing is, even with the time and help he's given me in the past, his office has never sent me a bill. Instead of paying me for things that my mother helped with, maybe you could ask your cousin to send me a bill for his services? I'm more worried about that, especially considering all the help I've been asking for recently."

"You're asking me to ask David to send you a bill for past legal services rendered?" Melanie asked. "I think you don't understand. It works the other way around, that clients ask him to maybe forget about sending a bill for his work."

"I know. It must sound rather silly to ask like that, but I still need to ask him for another favor, and I don't feel right about it unless I get square with what I owe."

"How long has it been since he helped you?"

"Several weeks." She thought of her car's tune up that lasted all day, and whatever he might've done to help Celeste last night. "He's done a lot for me."

"I wouldn't worry about it if it's been that long. What's the favor you need to ask him?" Melanie asked.

"There was a problem with some kahili stolen from the Kawaiaha'o Church, and when they were recovered, the only fingerprints on them were mine. But I don't ever remember handling them."

"I heard all about that from Thérèse, about how they were found in your room. Lucky you that your boyfriend was there at the time, a police officer, as a witness."

"Not my boyfriend," Maile hissed. "Anyway, I'm still in hot water over that."

"And you need David to represent you in court?"

"Not necessarily right away. I was talking to one of my tour guests today, a police evidence officer from Auckland, New Zealand. She does analysis of latent evidence, whatever that is. She said they're using something called Egyptian blue as a fingerprint dusting powder, and explained all about how it was able to find fingerprints that don't normally show up with the usual dust that police use."

"What's that got to do with David? He's not able to tell the police how to conduct their investigations. That could be construed as tampering with evidence," Melanie said.

"That's what my guest said. But I've been wondering if there was a way to get some of that special dust and have David request that an independent investigation be made looking for fingerprints other than mine? I looked online for the powder and the only stuff available was for official police use, and for laboratory studies."

"That's something that would be expensive. It would require a lot of time on his office's part, hiring a private investigator and an independent fingerprint forensic analysis expert to help. You're looking at some very big bills, Maile."

The air went out of Maile's chest. "That's what I figured. Thanks. I guess I'll just stick to claiming I'm innocent."

A moment passed before Melanie asked, "On another note, have you given any thought of coming to live and work as a nurse on Maui?"

"I still don't have my nursing license. It might be a few more months before I do, if they even give it back to me. That's why I'm still working as a tour guide."

"I see. You know, I have a friend named Bruce who is able to accomplish a lot of tasks."

"I don't want anything illegal done for me, Melanie. Or even to threaten anyone with something like that."

"It wouldn't be illegal. He works for a company I own, and I bet if anyone could find someone interested in helping you with your case, he could."

"I'd still have to pay, and we'd need the blue dust powder."

"If I tell Bruce something needs to get done, it gets done. It's a private security and intelligence company, and I bet they'd love to know more about this blue powder, just for their own database and use. And since I operate a private lab here on Maui, I might be able to purchase some of that powder."

"A medical lab?" Maile asked.

"Research lab. Don't forget I'm mayor of Maui and am responsible for the police department here. If we frame the purchase order correctly, I bet we could get some in a hurry."

"This is all sounding very expensive."

"Do you want your life back?" Melanie asked.

"Eventually."

"Give me a couple of days to see what I can learn about Egyptian blue and if it will help your case. If so, I'll have my guy Bruce arrange something to present to David. If he likes it, he'll present that to the District Attorney there in Honolulu. Who's the investigating detective?"

Maile almost hated the idea of volunteering his name. "Detective Ota. But he's been helpful to me, even letting me out on my own recognizance so I can work."

"David treads pretty lightly. He has political aspirations, so he has no choice about that."

"I keep forgetting who you guys are." For some reason, a tear ran down her cheek. "I can't believe I'm asking favors from a President's daughter and nephew."

"Never mind that. I'm just a local girl trying to make her way through life, just like you are, Maile. We need to look out for each other."

The exhaustion of the last few days, of the search for the stolen kahili, babysitting two energetic ten-year-olds, Lani's upside-down wedding, her arrest and subsequent jail fight, and finding Brock at the waterfall with Miss Wong, finally caught up with Maile when she turned off her light, casting her room into darkness.

Keepers of the Kingdom

Chapter Eighteen

When Wednesday morning rolled around, Maile still hadn't heard from Melanie Kato, David Melendez, or even from Detective Ota about her case. By the time her tours were done for the day and she sat down for dinner, she needed to talk to someone about the case of the kahili. Concerned about getting a giant bill from David, and not wanting to bother the mayor of another county, she called Detective Ota.

"Do you mind coming in to talk to me?" he asked.

"I know better than that, Detective. You're asking the chicken to leave the safety of the coop to enter the fox's den. Sorry, not this time. I'm just not interested in spending the night with Suzie Suzuki and her friends."

"What if I promise not to do that?"

"Half the time, you have one of your lackeys lock me up. Learned that lesson, also."

"You're not going to get locked up, not by me or anyone else. I have something to show you that should make you quite happy."

"You can't just tell me about it over the phone?"

"It'll more fun if you come in and see for yourself."

In a good mood, and the fun of Thanksgiving coming the next day, she felt compliant to his request. She also pried a promise out of him for a ride home afterward.

Taking the bus from the university to the downtown police station took only a few minutes. It was turning out to be a wet evening, with a steady rain falling ever since she bid her last tour group goodbye in the afternoon. The winter rainy season was starting in earnest. Stepping off the bus, she popped up her umbrella and dashed along the sidewalk to the police station. She was led from the front desk by a clerk through the maze of corridors to the squad room where she found Detective Ota at his desk. He wasn't alone.

"Oh, so that's what this is about," she muttered as she went to his desk. She tried not glaring at Brock, who was in uniform, discussing something about paperwork with Ota.

Brock nodded at her. "Ms. Spencer."

"Sergeant Turner."

"Maile, have a seat. Turner, get lost," Ota said, pushing a chair out for her with his foot. After Brock was gone, she sat next to Ota's desk, facing him. "What's with you two?"

"With who?" Maile asked, feigning innocence at the question.

"You and Turner. The two of you used to look at each other like puppies waiting to be fed, your tails wagging."

"Oh, him. He's a jerk. Ask him why."

"I intend to."

"Is that why you called me down here?"

He handed over full-page color enlargements for her to look at. On the prints were short sections of wood poles with shiny blue fingerprints along the shafts, with one set of black prints among all the others.

"What's this?" she asked, shuffling through the images.

"Proof of your innocence. You're looking at conclusive evidence you were not the last person to have handled the kahili before they arrived in your room."

"These are the poles that go with the kahili?"

"Right. I sent a team to the church yesterday to collect more evidence from the kahili. Reverend Akamu was quite gracious about it."

"Gracious almost to a fault." She sorted through the pages again. "Seriously, I don't know what I'm looking at."

"Look more closely. Those black fingerprints are yours. The glowing blue prints belong to someone else."

Maile looked more closely. What she found were her black prints overlaid with glowing blue prints. That wasn't the biggest question in her mind right then. "What's this blue color?"

"Something called Egyptian blue. It's a very fine powder, much finer than what most police departments use for lifting fingerprints, and it has luminescent properties that make prints show up under specific lighting conditions."

Maile did her best not to smile. "Oh? That sounds interesting. It this the latest technology in crime fighting?"

"The Maui Police Department used some on a case they had pending and found how useful it was. They sent us a batch of it, and our commander asked that we try it on a few outstanding cases. He even suggested I use it on the kahili that have been troubling you so much lately."

"That's rather convenient," she said.

"Sure is. I'm still trying to figure if there was more to it than mere coincidence."

"Please do me a favor and don't look too hard," she told him.

He tapped a pencil on his desk blotter. "I must admit, it worked great."

"Sure looks like it. There are a lot more prints on this than just mine." She peered closely at one set with her prints. "It almost looks like there are other fingerprints on top of mine. Wouldn't those be from the culprit?"

"Yes. Those were the last prints, the topmost ones on the poles, except for the ones added while taking them to the church that morning. Those belong to those two girls in your charge, Turner, two other groomsmen, and to you."

"Who do all the other prints belong to?" she asked.

"Some of them go way back, possibly years. The best preserved ones, and the uppermost ones, belong to two people. We've been able to identify one person, but the other is still pending."

"Well, go pick him up for questioning. Do you really say that, or is that only on TV?"

He gave her a questioning look and nodded. "We say it. But the problem is that since so many people have handled the kahili since then, I have no chain of evidence in their handling."

"But the last set of prints are from the people who stole the kahili! Go pick them up!"

"Can't use the prints as evidence in court. I know who to focus my investigation on, but that's as far as I can go. I need some other piece of evidence to bring them in for questioning," he said. He stacked the sheets and paper clipped them together.

"I had to sit in lockup and the real thieves go free?"

"You're not a hundred percent off the hook yet, at least not in the eyes of the DA. He still needs an explanation as to why your prints were on there."

"I've thought about that a hundred times since then. I have no idea why. I just don't remember ever handling those kahili."

"Is there a way you might've handled the poles without the feathers and other decorations on them?" he asked.

"I'm a tour guide, Detective, not a kung fu stick fighter or pole dancer. I just don't ever remember having any need or desire to touch those before the day of the wedding."

"Somehow you did handle them, and not all that long ago. Those prints were reasonably fresh, maybe only a few months old. A year, tops. Otherwise, they would've been too degraded to collect fingerprint powder."

"I wish I could help."

He cleared his desk, preparing to leave. "Still running with all this weather we're getting lately?"

"Not much choice, if I want to do well in the Honolulu Marathon in a few weeks."

"Thanksgiving is tomorrow. Big plans?"

"Pig out at my mom's house. She insists on finding the largest turkey on the planet. My auntie from Maui will be here. I haven't seen her in ages. Then Friday, I need to run off five-thousand calories of stuffing, yams, and cranberries. Tours all day on Saturday and Sunday."

"Sounds good."

"What about you? Do you and your wife entertain, or go to someone else's house?"

"Go elsewhere these last few years." He showed her to the sidewalk in front, where the rain was falling harder than ever. "Can you get home?"

"You promised me a ride."

"I need to go talk to a couple of witnesses before it gets too late. I trust you can get home on your own?"

"I have my bus pass. Hey, thanks for letting me see those pictures. That takes some of the pressure off."

"Try to remember when you might've handled those kahili before last Saturday. That would go a long way in keeping the DA, and me, off your back." He looked up the wet street. "Here comes your bus. Happy Thanksgiving, Ms. Spencer."

She thought of his message as she rode home, more of a command than a wish. Once she was home, she gave Lani a call for the first time since the wedding.

"Sistah Lani! Howzit! How's vacay at Disneyland going?"

"Wait." Maile listened as her friend went from one room to another, and some wind start in the background of the call. "Be more fun with a guy. Going on amusement park rides with my mom just isn't the same. I swear, she's gloomier than I am."

"Where are you?"

"On the balcony of the hotel."

"Not gonna jump?"

"Not today. But I swear to god, if my mother gives me one more lecture about men…"

Maile chuckled. "Yours and mine both. Maile filled her in on news of Honolulu, which wasn't much more than a weather report.

"What about Brock? Having him over for Thanksgiving?"

"I'd like to have him stuffed and baked, is what I'd like."

"What happened? I thought the two of you had your eyes all over each other, if not your hands?"

"Miss Wong is what happened," Maile hissed. She filled in a few of the details of finding them at the waterfall the weekend before.

"We have a Filipino word for guys like that."

"I think there's a word in every language. I have a few choice words to describe Miss Wong, also."

"Ha! I bet you do. Hey, my mom wants to go for our evening walk through the resort. I'll be home on Sunday. Call me."

***

On Thanksgiving morning, Maile decided to run to her mother's house. Kenny was picking up their aunt at the airport, which gave Maile the entire morning to get a long run. It was a drizzly morning, and being a holiday, the city was quiet. She had the sidewalk to herself as she went past her mother's cottage, barely giving it a look. No car was there and she hoped Kenny remembered to pick up their aunt at the airport. She continued up the road past the unavoidable Chinese cemetery before hitting the steeper portions that led into the arboretum. She left the sidewalk behind, leaving only a narrow strip of pavement for her to run on. There was no traffic now, and the forest was hers as she climbed, one soggy footstep at a time. The rain stopped once she was in the forest, turning to a heavy mist, giving her a chill.

She wasn't sure why she was running there that day. There was nothing cheerful about the scenery, the dense jungle of woods more dramatic than ever. Of all the sidewalks and paths that Honolulu had to offer, she was following one of the gloomiest, guaranteed wet and gray. Images of ancient Hawaiian warriors appearing as ghouls in the woods pranced through her mind. She tried chasing them away with more pedestrian ideas, which led to memories of Brock and Miss Wong playing at the waterfall. All things considered, the ghouls brought happier thoughts.

Maile focused on her running by tapping a fingertip on her sports watch. She tried remembering the turns in the road, and how much further the visitor center was. She could get a drink of water there, even if she wasn't thirsty. Another shiver hit, this one brought on by the sensation that she was being watched. She lengthened her stride and ran harder, now only wanting to get to her turn-around point and head back down.

The woods were dark, too dark for comfort when she arrived at the visitor center. She needed to decide if she wanted to add another mile and a half by doing some trail running to the falls. With no cars parked in the area, she was sure she'd have the trail, and the falls, to herself. Or at least she'd be the only mortal on the trail. The legend of Kahalaopuna she'd told the New Zealanders a few days before seemed more real than ever. The shiver than went through her body was the answer she needed.

Instead of stopping for even that short moment to catch a drink of water, she turned around and headed back down the hill to home. Memories of missed opportunities, legends of dead young women, and warrior ghouls just weren't the risk of entanglement.

Even though the running was easier, her mind was still playing tricks on her. Scanning the woods for something, anything, it felt as though the mist was closing in on her. Running even faster, she couldn't shake the sense of claustrophobia.

As Maile rounded a hairpin turn, rainwater drained across the road in a small torrent. Landing a step on a hidden rock sent her into a tumble. Righting herself again, and wiping smudges of mud from her legs, she looked to the sky.

"Lono! What'd I do to piss you off, anyway?"

In a few more minutes, she'd emerged from the mist and running along the straighter section of road. She counted the familiar houses and blocks, and in a few more minutes, she rounded the corner to her mother's cottage. One light shone in the window of the Manoa House next door, and an autumn wreath of tropical flowers and foliage from the garden already hung on the front door. A smaller decoration hung on her mother's door, one made from maile vines, cheerful hibiscus, two plumeria, and a single bird of paradise at the top. It was her mother's way of telling the world a family lived there.

A car was in the driveway, one she didn't recognize, the one Kenny borrowed that day. Instead of going in through the front door, she went around to the patio of the larger house next door and hosed herself off. A streak of blood from a scraped knee reached to her shoe. Washing that away, she could smell the turkey in the oven. Her next stop was at the large aviary in the backyard. She opened the screen door and went in.

Her pet cockatiel, King, squawked her name and fluttered to her arm. She rubbed his nose for a moment.

"Are you my king? Huh? Have you been a good king this week?" Thinking of the aroma of cooking turkey hanging in the air, she cooed at him again when he continued to flutter his wings. "Don't worry. We're not going to cook you. You're too skinny."

King squawked his loudest yet.

"Oh, really? Well, you can just go outside in the rain, if you're going to be that way."

She opened the door for him, where he hopped across the lawn to the flowerbeds looking for a meal. While he dined on whatever he found, Maile shoveled the floor of his pen and hosed everything down. Once she was done with his aviary, it was time to put him back again.

"Hey! Time to come home!"

She held the door open for him as he hopped into his home, going to the bowl of fresh feed she'd put out for him. He fluttered his wings to flick the rain off.

"What do you say to me? Huh? What do you say?"

King squawked something that sounded like her name, and that was good enough. When she went in the back door to the cottage, she found her mother and aunt there, making plans for something.

"Auntie Kelani! Howzit! You look as good as ever."

"Maile, how you get all wet?"

"Out for run."

"Your mother say you're running again. That's why you're so skinny. Trying for the Olympics?"

Maile got a drink of water. "I wish."

"Look like top athlete. Even arms getting muscles. Strong arms make you run faster?" Aunt Kelani asked.

Maile got a bottle of cold water from the fridge and took up a position of leaning in the doorway watching her mother prepare dinner. "Maybe a little. Just getting more exercise lately. Pushups, situps, that sort of thing."

"Skinned your knee, girl," her mother said. "Better put bandage on that after your shower."

"Yeah, Lono mad at me for something today."

"What about your friend, Kaniela?" her mother asked.

"What about him?"

Kelani instantly brightened. "You have a boyfriend named Daniel?"

"Not hardly."

"You didn't invite him here for dinner?" Kealoha asked.

"I called him, but he's working today."

"Who's Daniel?" Kelani insisted.

"One of the nurses where I used to work."

"Probably works too much," Kealoha said. "Needs spend time with friends. Poor boy. Afraid of so many things right now."

"What's wrong with Daniel?" Kelani asked.

"Nothing's wrong with Daniel," Maile said. "He's just had himself locked in a closet for so long, and now he's peeking through the gap, wondering if it's okay to come out."

"Closet?" Kelani asked.

"Mahu closet."

"Oh, that closet," her aunt said.

"Maile brought him to church. People liked him."

"I wonder?" Maile said. "I wonder if the congregation accepted him because he sat with us? Or if they'd have shunned him if he sat alone?"

"Not our business, girl. Peaceful congregation is our business. If people don't want to like each other, that's their problem to fix, not ours. Kaniela will make friends, if he's honest with them, and himself."

"Probably so. Where's Kenny?"

"Studying for finals next week."

She found her brother in his old room playing with his ancient Game Boy. "Done studying?"

"Still have time."

Maile grabbed one of his textbooks and tossed it at him.

"Hey! What'd you do that for?"

"Maybe only way to get knowledge in your head is to hit you with it."

After her shower, Maile put on full-length sweats, tops and bottoms, to warm up again. She found her aunt in the small living room that doubled as the dining room for guests on special occasions. She was on the couch looking at an old-fashioned scrapbook that her mother kept. They chatted about her failed marriage and how she'd lost her job at the hospital, and had turned to being a tour guide.

"How's your new Maui condo, Auntie? Where is it again?"

"Ka'anapali. Too big for just me. Why don't you come for visit? Plenty of room for you and a friend."

"You're trying to find out if I have a boyfriend, and the answer is no, I don't. Nice try, though."

"Come anyway. Maybe you'll find someone there."

"Just like mom. Ink barely dry on the divorce papers and already trying to get me married again."

"Not just married, trying to get you hapai family way."

"Still plenty of time for that."

Maile looked at the pictures in the scrapbook as her aunt turned pages. They were up to the Christmas season from the year before. There were pictures of them putting up the fake tree that had decorated the cottage since she was a girl, along with the childish decorations that she, and in turn Kenny, had fawned over as kids.

"We need to get a real tree this year, instead of that stupid old thing," Maile said.

Her mother had brought warm cider for them to drink, and even Kenny was in the room now that turkey dinner was close. "No more like that tree? What's wrong with it?"

"All falling apart and not even green anymore."

"Just needs more decorations, that's all."

"Needs a match, is what it needs," Kenny said.

"Maile tell you how she had help last week in watching the Kingdom?" Kealoha asked.

"Don't bring it up, Mom."

"About time you got help," Aunt Kelani said. "Big job keeping us all together."

Kenny snickered. "Getting little girls to help her."

After being pressured by her aunt, Maile told the story about the two girls that had spent the day with her, and their roles in the adventure of finding the missing kahili. "To make it more fun, I turned them into honorary princesses and Keepers of the Kingdom."

"One's even Hawaiian," Kealoha said when going back to the kitchen.

"Two drops in her veins," Maile muttered.

"Even just one drop enough to keep us alive."

Aunt Kelani turned a page to one of pictures of them at church. It wasn't their neighborhood church, but that of the Kawaiaha'o Church in town. The interior was being decorated by a dozen people hanging garlands from the balcony, and bringing in potted poinsettias. Several Christmas trees in various sizes were being decorated on either side of the altar. One of the kahili was in its usual place against the back wall, but the other was tilted and out of place.

With a closer look at the picture, she saw her mother vacuuming the floor behind the altar, right where that kahili should be. Looking even closer, she tried to figure out who it was holding the kahili by the pole. She wasn't sure, but the sweater the person was wearing looked familiar. The problem was that the picture had been taken from the balcony from the far side of the nave, the photographer trying to get as large of a field of view as possible of the interior as people decorated and cleaned. Because of that, no one in the picture was in clear focus.

"Mom!" She took the scrapbook from her aunt's hands and went to the kitchen. "Is this you vacuuming?"

Kealoha barely glanced at the picture. "Do I ever do anything else at the churches?"

"Being serious now. Who's this helping you?"

"That's you, girl. Don't you remember? We spent all morning cleaning our church, then went to Kawaiaha'o to clean there. All Keneka do all day is eat cookies people brought. Eat so many cookies, no more for anyone else."

"I don't care about the cookies. You're sure that's me holding the kahili like that?" Maile asked.

"Definitely you," Kealoha said after looking again. "You got that sweater as early gift from Robbie."

Maile took the scrapbook back. "Only gift I got from him last year."

Once she returned the book to her aunt, she went to her old bedroom in the cottage, now more of a sewing and quilting room for her mother. She still kept clothes there for when she stayed overnight. Digging through a box in the closet labeled as *Xmas clothes*, she found the sweater. She remembered it better now that she had it in her hands, because of the green Christmas stocking on the front, making it a contender for Ugly Christmas Sweater competitions. When she looked at the picture again, she saw what looked like could be one edge of the stocking.

"I kinda remember that day, and maybe helping Mom with the vacuuming," she said to no one in particular. She explained the mess of the investigation to her aunt, and how the police and District Attorney needed something to show how her fingerprints had gotten onto the poles of the Kahili. "But is that me?"

"Skinny girl, your size," her aunt said. "Long kind hair but too straight for you."

Being one-fourth Japanese, Maile's hair was straighter than her mother's, and darker. But it still fluffed up uncontrollably in high humidity. "Wait a minute."

When they were called to the table for dinner, Kenny almost ran, and was followed by Kelani. Maile brought up the rear, her phone in her hand, her thumb rapidly swiping across the screen in search of pictures from a year before.

"Maile girl, put phone away at the table," her mother commanded.

"But…"

"You know the rules. Away."

Putting her phone away, Maile scanned the table and saw all of her and Kenny's favorites. There was something new this year, though.

"No more poi? Guacamole for Thanksgiving?"

"Plenty of avocados to eat. Gotta do something with them."

"Not a kanaka Thanksgiving meal without poi," Kelani said. She sounded truly disappointed, even more so than Maile.

As man of the family, Kenny said grace. Serving bowls were passed around while Maile carved slices from the bird for plates. Kenny had to be told to slow down several times, and even Maile found herself eating too quickly at one point. All she wanted was to get back to her phone to search for images from the Christmas before.

"How was I wearing my hair last year?" Maile asked at one point.

"Same way as always," her mother said.

"I wasn't here," Aunt Kelani said.

"You changed it?" Kenny asked.

"Thanks for noticing, brah."

"Why so important?" her mother asked. "Gonna make change again?"

"Not today. I just need to know if that's me in the picture."

"You could try something new," her mother said, going after another slice of turkey. "Long time look like that."

"There's a girl in my condo, your age, cute what she does…"

"If you're looking for a guy, they like long hair," Kenny said.

"No, duh. And I'm not changing my hair for some guy. I just need to know when I straightened it, if it was before Christmas or after."

"Before," her mother said.

"After," Kenny said.

"I don't know. I wasn't here," Aunt Kelani muttered. "Good turkey, Sis. Always good with turkey."

"Good with ham, too," Kenny said. "Are we having ham at Christmas?"

"Doctor said no more ham," Kealoha said. "Maile girl, what's that stuff I have that's too high?"

"Cholesterol. Kenny, why do you think it was after Christmas?"

"What was after Christmas?"

"I straightened my hair?"

"You're still yapping about that?"

"I need to know, okay?"

"No fighting on Thanksgiving," her mother said. "Maile, eat more yams. Too skinny."

"Not too skinny." Maile watched as a spoon of candied yams was plunked onto her plate, followed by stuffing, both smothered with gravy. A new slice of turkey was put on the top. "I have to eat all that?"

Aunt Kelani added cubed potatoes to the plate. "Boys like girls with round butts, not flat ones."

"No butts at dinner table," Kealoha said.

"All this is growing one on me," Maile muttered, digging in. Once they were done and the leftovers removed, the pumpkin pie was brought out. They were all slumped in their chairs for comfort. "Pie already?"

"You can look at your phone if you eat pie," her mother said.

"Just half a slice," Maile said, slipping her phone from her pocket. She resumed where she left off in searching for pictures of herself from the year before. She looked up when a giant slice of warm, sweaty pie was put in front of her. She looked across the table at her brother's dessert. "Why's mine bigger than Kenny's?"

"Round butt, more dates," her aunt said.

"Round maybe, but not gigantic." Eating her pie slowly, she swiped from one picture to the next, still in search of a clear image of her taken before Christmas. "Nothing."

"Whatchu looking for?" her mother finally asked.

Maile sighed. "Looking for pictures of me taken before Christmas."

"For?"

"To see if I had straight hair."

"Humid kind days make your hair go poofy."

"I know, Mom. Been dealing with it for a long time."

"There's stuff you can put in it…" Aunt Kelani started to say.

"Why you want picture of straight hair?" Kealoha asked. "Just go get it if you want it that way."

"I need the picture to show the police, along with the picture in the scrapbook and the red and green sweater I got from Robbie."

"What picture in scrapbook?"

"Of you vacuuming and me…maybe me holding the kahili."

"Nobody care about who vacuumed the floor at church."

"I need…" Maile settled her voice. She knew that even if she explained again about the fingerprints on the poles, and how the pictures of the church being cleaned the year before were related, it would fall on deaf ears. "…the picture."

"For?"

"If I can prove to Detective Ota that that's me in the picture holding the kahili pole last year, then that would be the evidence he needs to know I handled the kahili sometime before they were stolen. But the picture in the scrapbook is too blurry to recognize me. It just shows a girl built like me with straight hair wearing a red and green sweater. No shortage of them in Honolulu."

"And if you show him a picture of you with straight hair and the sweater, that gets you off the hook?"

"Yes," Maile said, taking the last bite of her pumpkin pie.

"Why didn't you say so? I have pictures in my phone. Let me get." When her mother returned with her phone, she handed it over to Maile. "You know how it works better'n me."

Her mother didn't have nearly so many pictures, since Maile had ones of tour guests in hers, along with all the scenery shots she took. She quickly scrolled backwards through holiday gatherings until she got to the Christmas before. She stopped when she got to one of her in the backyard garden of the house next door, King perched on her arm being held aloft right after he'd come back from getting his wings clipped. In the picture, she was wearing the sweater. "This is what I need. I forgot all about this picture."

Her mother looked at the picture. "You got your hair done that same day as his wings got clipped. You even made joke about getting your hair clipped someday, like his wings. Never done it, though."

"One of these days," Maile said, arranging a folder in the phone.

"You still family barber?" Kelani asked.

"Not for me," Kenny said, now on his second slice of pie.

"Too proud for your mother to be your barber," Kealoha said. "How long since for you, Maile girl?"

"Since what?" Maile asked, still scrolling for more images of her in the sweater.

"Haircut."

"I don't know. Since I got married, I guess. Why?"

"Overdue. Not a kid anymore."

Maile tossed another image into the file. "Yours is longer."

"You'd look nice with something like mine," Aunt Kelani said.

Maile glanced up at her aunt's wash-and-go tidy style that barely reached her collar, the complete opposite of her mother's. "Not yet."

Ignoring the half slice of pie that was put on her empty plate, Maile got busy sending the file she'd made from her mother's phone to her own. Once that was done, she called Detective Ota. Listening to it ring a dozen times, she gave up.

"Who you calling?"

"The detective investigating the kahili."

"Thanksgiving. Good day to leave people alone."

Chapter Nineteen

The leftovers had been divided up, one part for Maile to take home, the other part for Kenny to take back to his dorm. As soon as they were on the road, she balled a fist and socked him in the arm.

"You little worm. Why'd you tell Auntie I'm dating someone?"

"Aren't you were seeing that cop?"

"Where'd you get that idea?"

"You're always hanging around together. In that wedding ceremony together. Everybody was talking about it. No big secret."

"Yeah, that's great, but he's seeing someone else."

"How am I supposed to know? Auntie kept asking questions. "

"You're supposed to keep your big trap shut, especially with Auntie. She's the biggest blabbermouth in the islands."

"You have tours to give tomorrow?" he asked.

"Sleeping in before going on a run. Then I'm going to the police station. Why?"

"Having trouble with chemistry. Can you help me figure it out?"

"What? You're a sophomore now, brah. Can't be messing around with classes anymore. You need to declare a major pretty soon. What is it, anyway?"

"That's something else you need to help me figure out."

"Hey, I'm done with school. You need to decide on your own major. If you want help with chem, I'll help with that. But don't come to me every time you get a D because you spend all your time on Game Boy."

He stopped the car in front of her building. "Might be getting an F."

"Brah! Who paid your tuition last quarter?"

"You did."

"And who did the work to earn that money?"

Kenny squirmed. "You did."

"And what does that mean?"

"I have to get better grades."

"Or what happens?" she asked.

"You pound me into an early grave."

"Very good." She pushed the car door open. "You just passed Professor Maile's logic class."

***

Friday was warm and sunny in the late morning when Maile woke. It had been more than a week that she'd heard anything come from her neighbor's apartment, and a month since she'd heard them argue. When she heard Rosamie come home from the grocery, she called her friend over.

"You've been wanting to talk to me for ages. Is today a good day? I have the kettle on the stove."

Rosamie beamed. "Be right over!"

When the neighbor sat at Maile's little table a few minutes later, she was clutching something in her hand. Maile had a good idea of wha it was.

"What's that?"

Rosamie handed over the medical image printout. "Gonna be a mother again."

"Oh, wow! Look at that! You sure are." Maile turned the ultrasound image one way and another. "You know if it's a boy or girl?"

"Still just a walnut."

"But it's there! I'm so happy!"

"Bad news, though," Rosamie said quietly, as though it were a secret.

"Uh oh. With the baby?"

Rosamie shook her head. "Gonna move one of these days. No more space over there for all of us. That's why hubby doing all the extra shifts, to earn money for down payment on a place of our own."

"On this island?"

"Hope so. Maybe back home to the Philippines."

"But you guys have been here for a long time. This is your home now."

"The Philippines will always be back home, even if we haven't been there in forever. Cheaper there."

"Better life here, isn't it? Isn't that why your families came here?"

Rosamie nodded. "Gotta stay busier to afford it, though."

"No kidding." Maile gave her friend a hug. "Whatever you do will be best. Just promise me you let me know ahead of time."

"Might take you with us!"

Already feeling a sense of loss over her friend moving away, Maile hit the road for a long run. This was on level ground through central Honolulu toward Kahala, roughly following the official marathon route. She didn't run the entire length, doing only half the distance. Some of her dinner from the day before was still working its way through her system, but it gave her the energy she needed. When she was done with one of her longest runs in ages, she took a nap. There was no putting off her trip to the police station any longer when she woke.

"Ota made it sound like he was going to be at the station today." She gave him a call and explained what she had to show him with the pictures at the church and her sweater. "Is that enough to change my status from suspect to witness?"

"You were only a person of interest, but yes. Do you have the pictures and sweater?"

"I have plenty of time to bring them in this afternoon, if you need to see everything together?" she offered.

"On a stakeout for the rest of the day, but if you take them in, someone else can take a look and log them into evidence."

"Will I get everything back?"

"After the trial."

"Yeah, but if you haven't even arrested anyone, how long will that be?"

"That's the stakeout. We're watching someone of interest related to that investigation."

"Toss him in a cell with Suzie. She'd pry a confession out of him, using her own special way."

Ota laughed. "She has a way with men."

"Who're you watching on today's stakeout? Am I allowed to ask that?"

"Usually, no. Especially you."

"Yes, I know. You don't want me interfering in your investigations."

"This has something to do with you. We're keeping an eye on your new friend, Fred the handyman."

"Why is he so interesting? All he did was put new locks on my door. Oh, I get it. He might still have keys to my room, and that makes him a suspect?"

"You're a good student, Maile. But what really makes him interesting to me is that two of the fingerprints on the kahili poles belong to him. Unfortunately, there are so many sets of prints on those things now, that most are smudged and difficult to identify."

"Sorry. I don't understand how his prints got on those poles?"

"Either do I, and that's why I'm watching him. And as a reminder, please don't leave the island."

Maile laughed. "When I do, you'll be one of the first to know!"

Taking the bus on a semi-holiday was a breeze. She had everything she needed in her bag to turn over to the police to get her off the police watch list. This week's, anyway. She had to wait at the front desk for a few minutes before an officer came to meet her.

"Oh, you," she said, when Brock came out.

"Does Detective Ota know you're here? Because he's not in right now."

"I already talked to him. He's on a stakeout." She held the bag with the sweater and pictures out to him. "He's expecting you to put these into evidence."

"What is all this?"

"Evidence that I handled the kahili poles before they showed up in my apartment. Supposedly that's good enough for him."

Brock had her follow him to the evidence room, where he logged them into evidence and gave her a receipt for them. He looked at the pictures and sweater and agreed they all went together to look like Maile.

"You're pretty with straight hair," he said.

"I'm not otherwise?"

"No, I mean straight hair is nice on you."

"Just like Miss Wong."

"Maile…"

"Sorry. Cheap shot. How was your Thanksgiving?"

He led her through corridors back to the front reception desk. "I worked."

"Was it busy?"

"Not really. A few of us were able to eat together."

"That's nice. Where?"

"At Chop…" He stalled mid-answer.

"Chop Suey City? Nice. You were able to spend it with Miss Wong. Wouldn't be the same without Detective Ota, though," she said.

"He was there."

"He was? He told me he was spending the day with his wife."

"His wife?" Brock asked.

"Yeah. It was a day off and he was spending it with his wife."

"I don't know what wife you're talking about, but Detective Ota's wife passed away a few years ago."

Maile was confused. "But he talks about going home from work to see his wife."

"His wife is buried in the Nu'uanu Cemetery. He goes there almost every day to visit her grave."

"I never knew."

"You might want to lay off his daughter, too."

"He has a daughter? I have no idea who she is."

"You know her quite well."

"I'm still trying to figure out why I never knew his wife had passed." Maile dug through her bag for her hat and sunglasses. "Anyway, I don't know any women named Ota."

"She uses her mother's maiden name."

"Seriously, tired of playing twenty questions with you."

"Suzuki, as in Susan Suzuki."

"Suzie is his daughter? Jailbait Suzie?" Maile scanned her memory for something. "I thought I heard her parents were both dead, that she was all alone in the world."

"From what I've heard, she's always been a handful. Then her mother died when she was barely a teenager. It wasn't long after then that she left home and got legal documents as an emancipated person. To her, he's no longer her father, just another cop making her life miserable."

"He said something the other day about her being an embarrassment for being in jail so often. He can't get her straightened out?" she asked.

Brock shook his head. "That's why he puts you in the cell with her."

"No, brah. He puts me in there until he can check witnesses and evidence."

"He doesn't care about any of that. He knows you're incapable of committing a crime worthy of arrest. He also knows you'd never flee the station if he left you alone at his desk."

"Why does he stick me in there with her? He knows it always leads to a fight."

"He's hoping you can be some sort of example to her, have a long talk with her."

"He can invite me to his house to talk with her, if that's what he wants."

"She wouldn't come. Putting you in the cage with her makes for a captive audience. Maybe next time, try not to get in a fight with her."

"Won't be a next time, brah. You and Ota can count of that."

"He'd appreciate it if you helped with his daughter."

"Why me?" she asked.

"He trusts you." Brock shrugged. "He likes you."

"What's that supposed to mean? He wants to date me, get married, and just so I can become Suzie's stepmother?"

"You're more of a daughter figure to him."

"Oh, now that's not weird at all."

"Just consider it, Maile."

***

With few errands to fill her day, Maile had time to take life at a strolling pace that day. She stopped at a flower store for a small bouquet and a lei. It was a slow bus ride up the Nu'uanu Valley to one of the many cemeteries that served Honolulu. The first one she went to was a modern place that rose up a gentle slope. Once she was there, she used their Wi-Fi to search a popular website for Mrs. Ota's grave. There were several Suzukis in the cemetery, but she found a woman's name who had been buried four years before.

"Louisa Suzuki Ota," she said, looking down at the gravestone once she found it. The picture of a pretty face of a Japanese woman looked from where it was sealed behind a window on the stone. A Buddhist emblem was carved on the marker, something common in Honolulu cemeteries. There was a small bouquet of cheerful yellow flowers in a reusable plastic vase stabbed into the ground next to the stone. Opposite of her name on the headstone was a blank space, ostensibly for Detective Ota's, when his time came. "You were only forty-eight years old."

She found another plastic vase and put her bouquet in the ground near the other. She said two quick prayers for the woman, one Christian, the other Hawaiian. It had been twenty years since her Japanese grandmother had died, so remembering one of the prayers she heard from her was impossible.

"Sorry. I don't know any Buddhist prayers. I hope one of mine was good enough."

It was a short walk to the Royal Mausoleum, the resting place of past Hawaiian monarchs. Going to one grave in particular, she laid her lei of maile vine on the low curb in front of the stone and said a prayer in Hawaiian. After, she remained there, looking at the massive monolith.

The wind that came over the Ko'olau Mountains was steady that day, bringing more rain clouds with it. Her loose blouse fluttered in the wind, as did her silk bandana around her neck. When hair blew across her face, she put it in a loose braid. There was no reason to cry right then, but she allowed a tear to roll down her cheek.

She thought of all the events of the last few days. There were the girls arriving on her doorstep that needed attention, and the missing kahili. She knew she'd risked the girls' safety by taking them on her search for the kahili, and then abandoned them with her mother, only to go on a scavenger hunt for kisses, from strangers of all things. She'd gotten maybe the two best kisses of her life from the brother of the man who almost became her lover, and hadn't heard from him since. Lani's heartbreak had been a blow to everyone, but she was slowly recovering with the help of her mother at the Happiest Place on Earth. Something that knocked her hard was seeing Brock and Miss Wong sharing a public moment of intimacy. Then came the revelation that Prince Aziz was somehow behind the kahili being stolen. Then there was Daniel coming out, to her anyway, and the news that Rosamie was expecting another baby. All that in barely a week, and in one way or another, she was a part of all of it.

She focused on the monolith that celebrated the memory of her ancestors.

"Not a very good keeper of the kingdom, am I?"

As the wind tugged at her clothes and fluttered the simple kerchief around her neck, she got a sudden urge.

...

More from Kay Hadashi

Maile Spencer Honolulu Tour Guide Mysteries
AWOL at Ala Moana
Baffled at the Beach
Coffee in the Canal
Dead on Diamond Head
Honey of a Hurricane
Keepers of the Kingdom
Malice in the Palace
Peril at the Potluck

Gina Santoro Mysteries
Unknown Victim
Hidden Agenda
And more!

The June Kato Intrigue Series
Kimono Suicide
Stalking Silk
Yakuza Lover
Deadly Contact
Orchids and Ice
Broken Protocol

The Island Breeze Series

Island Breeze
Honolulu Hostage
Maui Time
Big Island Business
Adrift
Molokai Madness
Ghost of a Chance

Keepers of the Kingdom

The Melanie Kato Adventure Series
Away
Faith
Risk
Quest
Mission
Secrets
Future
Kahuna
Directive
Nano

The Maui Mystery Series
A Wave of Murder
A Hole in One Murder
A Moonlit Murder
A Spa Full of Murder
A Down to Earth Murder
A Haunted Murder
A Plan for Murder
A Misfortunate Murder
A Quest for Murder
A Game of Murder

The Honolulu Thriller Series
Interisland Flight
Kama'aina Revenge
Tropical Revenge
Waikiki Threat
Rainforest Rescue

Made in the USA
Columbia, SC
10 January 2025